Stumbling Through Life

Ruskin Bond is known for his signature simplistic and witty writing style. He is the author of several bestselling short stories, novellas, collections, essays and children's books; and has contributed a number of poems and articles to various magazines and anthologies. At the age of twenty-three, he won the prestigious John Llewellyn Rhys Prize for his first novel, *The Room on the Roof*. He was also the recipient of the Padma Shri in 1999, Lifetime Achievement Award by the Delhi Government in 2012, and the Padma Bhushan in 2014.

Born in 1934, Ruskin Bond grew up in Jamnagar, Shimla, New Delhi and Dehradun. Apart from three years in the UK, he has spent all his life in India, and now lives in Landour, Mussoorie, with his adopted family.

RUSKIN
BOND
Stumbling Through Life

RUPA

Published by
Rupa Publications India Pvt. Ltd 2018
7/16, Ansari Road, Daryaganj
New Delhi 110002

Sales centres:
Allahabad Bengaluru Chennai
Hyderabad Jaipur Kathmandu
Kolkata Mumbai

ISBN: 978-93-530-404-20

First impression 2018

10 9 8 7 6 5 4 3 2 1

CONTENTS

INTRODUCTION

Try. Fail. Try again. Fail again.

Try once more!

That just about sums up my life. A series of failures leading up to a modicum of success.

Today we hear of smart young writers turning out instant bestsellers, their books selling in hundreds of thousands. For many years I considered myself lucky if my books were being published at all.

Now writers become celebrities. Their books are marketed like Maggi noodles. They pour from the presses like popcorn from a vending machine. Literary festivals take place in hundreds of towns and cities, and the politicians gleefully attend them.

Although I have yet to read everything by Camus, Orwell and Agatha Christie, my spare table is overflowing with new books sent to me by authors, publishers and well-wishers who wish to improve my mind. Some even solicit my comments—and give me a deadline for doing so!

I will never read all these books. What will I do with them? The pile grows higher every day.

Gautam, who has just finished school, has come up with a solution. 'Whenever I go out,' he says, 'I'll take one or two books with me, and leave them in cafés or dhabas or on park benches. That way someone may pick them up—and even read them. Literature will spread like wildfire!'

So, I fell in with his idea, gave him a little pocket money (to spend in the cafés), and off he went his quota of books.

This quota of procedure was followed for several days, and the pile of unsolicited books was rapidly diminishing. So, I thought I'd take a look for myself and see how things were going.

Gautam had left a book on a bench just down the road from our flat. I stood behind a tree, and presently two ladies came along and pushing the book aside, sat down and exchanged the day's gossip for about fifteen minutes before getting up and leaving. They did not even glance at the book.

Five minutes passed. Then a monkey arrived on the bench, picked up the book, bit into it to see if it was edible, spat some of it out, and then tore it in two.

After the monkey had gone, along came two small boys. They seized the scattered pages, turned them into paper airplanes, and gleefully sent them flying over the valley.

Finally I wandered down to the bench to examine the remains of the book. The cover was still intact. I picked it up. And to my horror I saw that it was by Ruskin Bond!

Where's that boy, Gautam? No more pocket money for a week.

Ruskin Bond
23 March 2018

ON THE LOSS OF SOLITUDE AND MY PYJAMAS!

A little solitude now and then is good for the soul and good for the pen.

And it is not only writers who need it. We could all do with a few hours of solitary confinement—not in a jail cell but in a room or quiet corner of our own choice. How else can we get to know ourselves?

Not everyone is in a position to renounce the material world and live in a humble dwelling on the banks of the Ganga above Rishikesh, there to meditate and ponder upon the meaning or the lack of it in our transitory existence in a world that has been mismanaged by its human tenants. Children have to be fed, marriages brokered, and cars topped up with petrol. The great saints and sages looked to the mountains. The great poets and prose-writes—Tagore, Wordsworth, Stevenson, Melville, Conrad—turned to the rivers, lakes, seas and oceans. The mountains are static, but water is always on the move, there is no stopping it.

Solitude. The solitude of mountains, the solitude of the sea.

Probably the best work on solitude was Defoe's *Robinson*

Crusoe. Here was an intelligent man who, shipwrecked upon an uninhabited island, had solitude forced upon him. Most men would have gone mad after a year or two of complete isolation. But Crusoe learnt to adapt to the conditions and even appreciate his enforced solitude. The arrival of Man Friday proved at first to be unsettling, but their chemistry proved to be just right, and loneliness became companionship.

Solitude is a condition appreciated only by a small minority. It seems to me that most people are scared of being left on their own, for almost every human activity is carried out on a crowded scale.

As a boy, inspired by Thoreau's *Walden*, I sought out a Walden pond for myself, and discovered a wilderness outside Dehra Dun where a hot spring emerged from a dry riverbed. I would go there often on my bicycle. There were no other visitors, just occasionally a village boy grazing his cows.

Last year, I visited this same spot, although no longer on a bicycle. Hotels, restaurants, a veritable bazaar had come up on the banks of a tiny stream, but of the original hot spring there was no sign. In shock, it had probably gone underground.

In order to protect yourself from solitude or finding yourself on your own you can now equip yourself with a 'selfie' and take pictures of yourself with waterfalls and cheering crowds in the background; but take care that you don't step backwards into the waterfalls.

Strongly along the road below my mountain home I encountered a smart young person who wanted to take a picture of both of us with her selfie. I could hardly object. So we sat on the parapet, cheek to cheek, while she attempted to get us both into the fame of her camera. All she got was her pretty left ear and my red nose, but I didn't mind, it was a long time since I'd sat cheek to cheek with a pretty young thing on a parapet wall. There's something to be said for selfies!

And so I take issue with the gentleman on a TV programme who maintained that selfies were a form of narcissism, denoting some sort of psychological deficiency in the owners make-up. To me, they appear to be quite harmless few things, provided you don't fall off a cliff or a high-rise building.

The mirror—especially that dressing-table mirror—is probably the most additive form of narcissism and it's been around for centuries.

'Get away from that mirror!' my aunt would scream at me whenever I lingered in front of it for several minutes, trying my best to train my hair into a puff similar to the one sported by Dev Anand or Alan Ladd or whoever was the big male star that year. Nowadays you don't see stars with puffs, possibly because they go bald rather early. Must be all this pollution.

But to return to solitude, the only place where I can find it is in my own small room looking out over the mountains. But even here I must keep my windows closed if I am not to be joined by the monkeys.

There's one particular monkey that's been looking at me speculatively through the window glass all morning. Being short-sighted I can't tell if it's a male or female, but it makes no difference, they all have a strange desire to make off with my pyjamas. Is it because I like brightly-coloured pyjamas? Or is it some sort of Freudian simian obsession which can only be explained by that psychologist on the TV channel?

Anyway, my pyjamas disappear at the rate of one a month. I have only to leave the window open for half a minute, and away goes my pyjama, over the trees and far away.

There must be a part of the forest where a whole tribe of rhesus monkeys is prancing around in my many-coloured pyjamas. They are probably having their own fashion show.

RUNNING FOR COVER

The right to privacy is a fine concept and might actually work in the West, but in Eastern lands it is purely notional. If I want to be left alone, I have to be a shameless liar—pretend that I am out of town or, if that doesn't work, announce that I have measles, mumps or some new variety of Asian flu.

Now I happen to like people and I like meeting people from all walks of life. If this were not the case, I would have nothing to write about. But I don't like too many people all at once. They tend to get in the way. And if they arrive without warning, banging on my door while I am in the middle of composing a poem or writing a story, or simply enjoying my afternoon siesta, I am inclined to be snappy or unwelcoming. Occasionally I have even turned people away.

As I get older, that afternoon siesta becomes more of a necessity and less of an indulgence. But it's strange how people love to call on me between two and four in the afternoon. I suppose it's the time of day when they have nothing to do.

'How do we get through the afternoon?' one of them will say.

'I know! Let's go and see old Ruskin. He's sure to entertain us with some stimulating conversation, if nothing else.' Stimulating conversation in mid-afternoon? Even Socrates would have baulked at it.

'I'm sorry I can't see you today,' I mutter. 'I don't feel at all well.' (In fact, extremely unwell at the prospect of several strangers gaping at me for at least half-an-hour.)

'Not well? We're so sorry. My wife here is a homoeopath.'

It's amazing the number of homoeopaths who turn up at my door. Unfortunately they never seem to have their little powders on them, those miracle cures for everything from headaches to hernias.

The other day a family burst in—uninvited of course. The husband was an ayurvedic physician, the wife was a homoeopath (naturally), the eldest boy a medical student at an allopathic medical college.

'What do you do when one of you falls ill?' I asked, 'Do you try all three systems of medicine?'

'It depends on the ailment,' said the young man. 'But we seldom fall ill. My sister here is a yoga expert.'

His sister, a hefty girl in her late twenties (still single), looked more like an all-in wrestler than a supple yoga practitioner. She looked at my tummy. She could see I was in bad shape.

'I could teach you some exercises,' she said. 'But you'd have to come to Ludhiana.'

I felt grateful that Ludhiana was a six-hour drive from Mussoorie.

'I'll drop in some day,' I said. 'In fact, I'll come and take a course.'

We parted on excellent terms. But it doesn't always turn out that way.

There was this woman, very persistent, in fact downright rude, who wouldn't go away even when I told her I had bird flu.

'I have to see you,' she said, 'I've written a novel, and I want you to recommend it for a Booker Prize.'

'I'm afraid I have no influence there,' I pleaded. 'I'm

completely unknown in Britain.'

'Then how about the Nobel Prize?'

I thought about that for a minute. 'Only in the science field,' I said. 'If it's something to do with genes or stem cells?'

She looked at me as though I was some kind of worm. 'You are not very helpful,' she said.

'Well, let me read your book.'

'I haven't written it yet.'

'Well, why not come back when it's finished? Give yourself a year—two years—these things should never be done in a hurry.' I guided her to the gate and encouraged her down the steps.

'You are very rude,' she said. 'You did not even ask me in. I'll report you to Khushwant Singh. He's a friend of mine. He'll put you in his column.'

'If Khushwant Singh is your friend,' I said, 'why are you bothering with me? He knows all the Nobel and Booker Prize people. All the important people, in fact.'

I did not see her again, but she got my phone number from someone, and now she rings me once a week to tell me her book is coming along fine. Any day now, she's going to turn up with the manuscript.

Casual visitors who bring me their books or manuscripts are the ones I dread most. They ask me for an opinion, and if I give them a frank assessment they resent it. It's unwise to tell a would-be writer that his memoirs or novel or collected verse would be better off unpublished. Murders have been committed for less. So I play safe and say, 'Very promising. Carry on writing.' But this is fatal. Almost immediately I am asked to write a foreword or introduction, together with a letter of recommendation to my publisher—or any publisher of standing. Unwillingly I become a literacy agent; unpaid of course.

I am all for encouraging the arts and literature, but I do

think writers should seek out their own publishers and write their own introductions.

The perils of doing this sort of thing was illustrated when I was prevailed upon to write a short introduction to a book about a dreaded man-eater who had taken a liking to the flesh of the good people of Dogadda, near Lansdowne. The author of the book could hardly write a decent sentence, but he managed to string together a lengthy account of the leopard's depredations. He was so persistent, calling on me or ringing me up, that I finally did the introduction. He then wanted me to edit or touch up his manuscript; but this I refused to do. I would starve if I had to sit down and rewrite other people's books. But he prevailed upon me to give him a photograph.

Months later, the book appeared, printed privately of course. And there was my photograph, and a photograph of the dead leopard after it had been hunted down. But the local printer had got the captions mixed up. The dead animal's picture earned the line: 'Well-known author Ruskin Bond.' My picture carried the legend: 'Dreaded man-eater, shot after it had killed its 26th victim.'

The printer's devil had turned me into a serial killer.

Now you know why I'm wary of writing introductions.

'Vanity' publishers thrive on writers who are desperate to see their work in print. They will print and deliver a book at your doorstep and then leave you with the task of selling it; or to be more accurate, disposing of it.

One of my neighbours, Mrs Santra—may her soul rest in peace—paid a publisher forty thousand rupees to bring out a fancy edition of her late husband's memoirs. During his lifetime he'd been unable to get it published, but before he died he got his wife to promise that she'd publish it for him. This she did, and the publisher duly delivered 500 copies to the good lady.

She gave a few copies to friends, and then passed away, leaving the books behind. Her heir is now saddled with 450 hardbound volumes of unsaleable memoirs.

I have always believed that if a writer is any good he will find a publisher who will print, bind, and sell his books, and even give him a royalty for his efforts. A writer who pays to get published is inviting disappointment and heartbreak.

Many people are under the impression that I live in splendour in a large mansion, surrounded by secretaries and servants. They are disappointed to find that I live in a tiny bedroom-cum-study and that my living room is so full of books that there is hardly space for more than three or four visitors at a time.

Sometimes thirty to forty schoolchildren turn up, wanting to see me. I don't turn away children, if I can help it. But if they come in large numbers I have to meet and talk to them on the road, which is inconvenient for everyone.

If I had the means, would I live in a splendid mansion in the more affluent parts of Mussoorie, with a film star or TV personality as my neighbour? I rather doubt it. All my life I've been living in one or two rooms and I don't think I could manage a bigger establishment. True, my extended family takes up another two rooms, but they see to it that my working space is not violated. And if I am hard at work (or fast asleep) they will try to protect me from unheralded or unwelcome visitors.

And I have learnt to tell lies. Especially when I'm asked to attend school functions as a chief guest or in some formal capacity. To spend two or three hours listening to speeches (and then being expected to give one) is my idea of hell. It's hell for the students and it's hell for me. The speeches are usually followed (or preceded) by folk dances, musical interludes or class plays, and this only adds to the torment. Sports days are just as bad. You can skip the speeches (hopefully), but you must sit out in the hot sun for the greater part of the day, while a loudspeaker informs you that little Parshottam has just broken the school record for the under-nine high jump, or that Pamela Highjinks has won the hurdles for the third year running. You don't get to see the events because you are kept busy making polite conversation with the other guests. The only occasion when a sports' event really came to life was when a misdirected discus narrowly missed decapitating the headmaster's wife.

Former athletes and sportsmen seldom visit me. They have difficulty making it up my steps. Most of them have problems with their knees before they are fifty. They hobble (for want of a better word). Once their playing days are over, they start hobbling. Nandu, a former tennis champion, can't make it up my steps, nor can Chand—a former wrestler. Too much physical activity when young has resulted in an early breakdown of the body's machinery. As Nandu says, 'Body can't take it any more.' I'm not too agile either, but then, I was never much of a sportsman. Second last in the marathon was probably my most memorable achievement.

Oddly enough, some of the most frequent visitors to my humble abode are honeymooners.

Why, I don't know, but they always ask for my blessing even though I am hardly an advertisement for married bliss. A seventy-year-old bachelor blessing a newly married couple? Maybe they are under the impression that I'm a Brahmachari? But how would that help them? They are going to have babies sooner or later.

It is seldom that they happen to be readers or book lovers, so why pick an author, and that too one who does not go to places of worship? However, since these young couples are inevitably attractive, and full of high hopes for their future and the future of mankind, I am happy to talk to them, wish them well...and if it's a blessing they want, they are welcome. My hands are far from being saintly but at least they are well-intentioned.

I have, at times, been mistaken for other people.

'Are you Mr Pickwick?' asked a small boy. At least he'd been reading Dickens. 'A distant relative,' I said, and beamed at him in my best Pickwickian manner.

I am at ease with children, who talk quite freely except when accompanied by their parents. Then it's mum and dad who do all the talking.

'My son studies your book in school,' said one fond mother, proudly exhibiting her ten-year-old. 'He wants your autograph.'

'What's the name of the book you're reading?' I asked.

'*Tom Sawyer*,' he said promptly.

So I signed Mark Twain in his autograph book. He seemed quite happy.

A schoolgirl asked me to autograph her maths textbook.

'But I failed in maths,' I said. 'I'm just a story writer.'

'How much did you get?'

'Four out of a hundred.'

She looked at me rather crossly and snatched the book away.

I have signed books in the names of Enid Blyton, R.K. Narayan, Ian Botham, Daniel Defoe and J.K. Rowling. No one seems to mind.

ADVENTURES IN READING

1
BEAUTY IN SMALL BOOKS

You don't see them so often now, those tiny books and almanacs—genuine pocketbooks—once so popular with our parents and grandparents; much smaller than the average paperback, often smaller than the palm of the hand. With the advent of coffee-table books, new books keep growing bigger and bigger, rivalling tombstones! And one day, like Alice after drinking from the wrong bottle, they will reach the ceiling and won't have anywhere else to go. The average publisher, who apparently believes that large profits are linked to large books, must look upon these old miniatures with amusement or scorn. They were not meant for a coffee table, true. They were meant for true book lovers and readers, for they took up very little space—you could slip them into your pocket without any discomfort, either to you or to the pocket.

I have a small collection of these little books, treasured over the years. Foremost is my father's prayer book and psalter, with his name, 'Aubrey Bond, Lovedale, 1917', inscribed on the inside back cover. Lovedale is a school in the Nilgiri Hills in south India, where, as a young man, he did his teacher's training. He gave it to me soon after I went to a boarding school in Shimla in 1944, and my own name is inscribed on it in his beautiful handwriting.

Another beautiful little prayer book in my collection is called *The Finger Prayer Book*. Bound in soft leather, it is about the same length and breadth as the average middle finger. Replete with psalms, it is the complete book of common prayer and not an abridgement; a marvel of miniature book production.

Not much larger is a delicate item in calf-leather, *The Humour of Charles Lamb*. It fits into my wallet and often stays there. It has a tiny portrait of the great essayist, followed by some thirty to forty extracts from his essays, such as this favourite of mine: 'Every dead man must take upon himself to be lecturing me with his odious truism, that "Such as he is now, I must shortly be". Not so shortly friend, perhaps as thou imaginest. In the meantime, I am alive. I move about. I am worth twenty of thee. Know thy betters!'

No fatalist, Lamb. He made no compromise with Father Time. He affirmed that in age we must be as glowing and tempestuous as in youth! And yet Lamb is thought to be an old-fashioned writer.

Another favourite among my 'little' books is *The Pocket Trivet: An Anthology for Optimists*, published by *The Morning Post* newspaper in 1932. But what is a trivet? the unenlightened may well ask. Well, it's a stand for a small pot or kettle, fixed securely over a grate. To be right as a trivet is to be perfectly right. Just right, like the short sayings in this book, which is further enlivened by a number of charming woodcuts based on the seventeenth-century originals; such as the illustration of a moth hovering over a candle flame and below it the legend—'I seeke mine owne hurt.'

But the sayings are mostly of a cheering nature, such as Emerson's 'Hitch your wagon to a star!' or the West Indian proverb: 'Every day no Christmas, an' every day no rainy day.'

My book of trivets is a happy example of much concentrated wisdom being collected in a small space—the beauty separated from the dross. It helps me to forget the dilapidated building in which I live and to look instead, at the ever-changing cloud patterns as seen from my bedroom windows. There is no end to the shapes made by the clouds, or to the stories they set off in my head. We don't have to circle the world in order to find beauty and fulfilment. After all, most of living has to happen in the mind. And, to quote one anonymous sage from my trivet, 'The world is only the size of each man's head.'

2
WRITTEN BY HAND

Amongst the current fraternity of writers, I must be that very rare person—an author who actually writes by hand!

Soon after the invention of the typewriter, most editors and publishers understandably refused to look at any mansucript that was handwritten. A decade or two earlier, when Dickens and Balzac had submitted their hefty manuscrips in longhand, no one had raised any objection. Had their handwriting been awful, their manuscripts would still have been read. Fortunately for all concerned, most writers, famous or obscure, took pains over their handwriting. For some, it was an art in itself, and many of those early manuscripts are a pleasure to look at and read.

And it wasn't only authors who wrote with an elegant hand. Parents and grandparents of most of us had distinctive styles of their own. I still have my father's last letter, written to me when I was at boarding school in Shimla some fifty years ago. He used large, beautifully formed letters, and his thoughts seemed to have the same flow and clarity as his handwriting.

In his letter he advises me (then a nine-year-old) about my own handwriting; 'I wanted to write before about your writing. Ruskin...sometimes I get letters from you in very small writing, as if you wanted to squeeze everything into one sheet of letter paper. It is not good for you or for your eyes, to get into the habit of writing too small... Try and form a larger style of handwriting—use more paper if necessary!'

I did my best to follow his advice, and I'm glad to report that after nearly forty years of the writing life, most people can still read my handwriting!

Word processors are all the rage now, and I have no objection to these mechanical aids any more than I have to my old Olympia typewriter, made in 1956 and still going strong. Although I do all my writing in longhand, I follow the conventions by typing a second draft. But I would not enjoy my writing if I had to do it straight on to a machine. It isn't just the pleasure of writing longhand. I like taking my notebooks and writing pads to odd places. This particular essay is being written on the steps of my small cottage facing Pari Tibba (Fairy Hill). Part of the reason for sitting here is that there is a new postman on this route, and I don't want him to miss me.

For a freelance writer, the postman is almost as important as a publisher. I could, of course, sit here doing nothing, but as I have pencil and paper with me, and feel like using them, I shall write until the postman comes and maybe after he has gone too! There is really no way in which I could set up a word processor on these steps.

There are a number of favourite places where I do my

writing. One is under the chestnut tree on the slope above the cottage. Word processors were not designed keeping mountain slopes in mind. But armed with a pen (or pencil) and paper, I can lie on the grass and write for hours. On one occasion, last month, I did take my typewriter into the garden, and I am still trying to extricate an acorn from under the keys, while the roller seems permanently stained yellow with some fine pollen-dust from the deodar trees.

My friends keep telling me about all the wonderful things I can do with a word processor, but they haven't got around to finding me one that I can take to bed, for that is another place where I do much of my writing—especially on cold winter nights, when it is impossible to keep the cottage warm.

While the wind howls outside, and snow piles up on the windowsill, I am warm under my quilt, writing pad on my knees, ballpoint pen at the ready. And if, next day, the weather is warm and sunny, these simple aids will accompany me on a long walk, ready for instant use should I wish to record an incident, a prospect, a conversation, or simply a train of thought.

When I think of the great eighteenth- and nineteenth-century writers, scratching away with their quill pens, filling hundreds of pages every month, I am amazed to find that their handwriting did not deteriorate into the sort of hieroglyphics that often make up the average doctor's prescription today. They knew they had to write legibly, if only for the sake of the typesetters.

Both Dickens and Thackeray had good, clear, flourishing styles. (Thackeray was a clever illustrator too.) Somerset Maugham had an upright, legible hand. Churchill's neat handwriting never wavered, even when he was under stress. I like the bold, clear, straightforward hand of Abraham Lincoln;

it mirrors the man. Mahatma Gandhi, another great soul who fell to the assassin's bullet, had many similarities of both handwriting and outlook.

Not everyone had a beautiful hand. King Henry VIII had an untidy scrawl, but then, he was not a man of much refinement. Guy Fawkes, who tried to blow up the British Parliament, had a very shaky hand. With such a quiver, no wonder he failed in his attempt! Hitler's signature is ugly, as you would expect. And Napoleon's doesn't seem to know where to stop; how much like the man!

I think my father was right when he said handwriting was often the key to a man's character, and that large well-formed letters went with an uncluttered mind. Florence Nightingale had a lovely handwriting, the hand of a caring person. And there were many like her, amongst our forebears.

3
WORDS AND PICTURES

When I was a small boy, no Christmas was really complete unless my Christmas stocking contained several recent issues of my favourite comic paper. If today my friends complain that I am too voracious a reader of books, they have only these comics to blame; for they were the origin, if not of my tastes in reading, then certainly of the reading habit itself.

I like to think that my conversion to comics began at the age of five, with a comic strip on the children's page of *The Statesman*. In the late 1930s, Benji, whose head later appeared only on the Benji League badge, had a strip to himself; I don't remember his adventures very clearly, but every day (or was it once a week?) I would cut out the Benji strip and paste it into a scrapbook. Two years later, this scrapbook, bursting with the adventures of Benji, accompanied me to boarding school, where, of course, it passed through several hands before finally passing into limbo.

Of course comics did not form the only reading matter that found its way into my Christmas stocking. Before 1 was eight, I had read Peter Pan, Alice, and most of *Mr Midshipman Easy*; but I had also consumed thousands of comic papers which were, after all, slim affairs and mostly pictorial, 'certain little penny books radiant with gold and rich with bad pictures', as Leigh Hunt described the children's papers of his own time.

But though they were mostly pictorial, comics in those days did have a fair amount of reading matter too. *The Hostspur, Wizard, Magnet* (a victim of the Second World War) and *Champion* contained stories woven around certain popular characters. In *Champion*, which I read regularly right through my prep school years, there was Rockfist Rogan, Royal Air Force (R.A.F.), a pugilist who managed to combine boxing with bombing, and Fireworks Flynn, a footballer who always scored the winning goal in the last two minutes of play.

Billy Bunter has, of course, become one of the immortals—almost a subject for literary and social historians. Quite recently, *The Times Literary Supplement* devoted its first two pages to an analysis of the Bunter stories. Eminent lawyers and doctors still look back nostalgically to the arrival of the weekly *Magnet*; they are now the principal customers for the special souvenir edition of the first issue of the *Magnet*, recently reprinted in facsimile. Bunter, 'forever young', has become a folk hero. He is seen on stage, screen and television, and is even quoted in the House of Commons.

From this, I take courage. My only regret is that I did not preserve my own early comics—not because of any bibliophilic value which they might possess today, but because of my sentimental regard for early influences in art and literature.

The first venture in children's publishing, in 1774, was a comic of sorts. In that year, John Newberry brought out:

According to Act of Parliament (neatly bound and gilt): A Little Pretty Pocket-Book, intended for the Instruction and Amusement of Little Master Tommy and Pretty Miss Polly, with an agreeable Letter to read from Jack the Giant-Killer...

The book contained pictures, rhymes and games. Newberry's characters and imaginary authors included Woglog the Giant, Tommy Trip, Giles Gingerbread, Nurse Truelove, Peregrine Puzzlebrains, Primrose Prettyface, and many others with names similar to those found in the comic papers of our own century.

Newberry was also the originator of the 'Amazing Free Offer', so much a part of American comics. At the beginning of 1755, he had this to offer:

Nurse Truelove's New Year Gift, or the Book of Books for children, adorned with cuts and designed as a present for every little boy who would become a great man and ride upon a fine horse; and to every little girl who would become a great woman and ride in a Lord Mayor's gilt coach. Printed for the author, who has ordered these books to be given gratis to all little boys in St. Paul's churchyard, they paying for the binding, which is only two pence each book.

Many of today's comics are crude and, like many television serials, violent in their appeal. But I did not know American comics until I was twelve, and by then, I had become quite discriminating. Superman, Bulletman, Batman, Green Lantern, and other superheroes all left me cold. I had, by then, passed into the world of real books but the weakness for the comic strip remains. I no longer receive comics in my Christmas stocking; but I do place a few in the stockings of Gautam and Siddharth. And, needless to say, I read them right through beforehand.

BE PREPARED!

With Holi just around the corner I must remember to keep a couple of buckets of water ready—not coloured water, but plain and simple tap water so that, when all the revelry and colour play is over, I can take a bath.

You see, last year, when all the fun was over and the drums had ceased to beat, I made for the bathroom so that I could bathe and be recognizable again—only to find that the taps had run dry!

Not a drop of water in the house. And my neighbour was in the same predicament. We had to wait till late in the evening before a water-tanker arrived to relieve the situation.

So now, like a good Boy Scout, I shall be 'well-prepared'. That's the old Scouts motto in case you have forgotten. 'Be prepared!' I shall have my buckets of water ready just in case the taps run dry again. I'm not a fanatic about bathing but it won't do for me to turn up at the Cambridge Book Depot looking as though I've just fallen into a paintbox. 'Old Bond is finally going round the bend,' I can hear someone say. 'Now he's signing colouring books!'

So why play Holi at all? Well, there's a lot of goodwill involved in it, and I hate being a spoilsport. So why not join the merry throng and let my hair down for an hour or two?

Also, it's safer to run with the crowd than to run from it!

◆

More people on planet Earth means more water shortages. And other shortages too.

When Edison invented the electric bulb, everyone predicted that it would spell the end of the candle industry. But candles are everywhere. Our power shortages have seen to that.

Now everyone keeps a supply of candles. And if you run short you can go down the road and get as many as you want—ranging from small birthday-cake candles to candles as large cricket bats, guaranteed to last a week.

Candle-making is both an art and an industry. Only last month we were informed (via the TV channels) that a certain politician, sent to jail, was immediately put to work making candles. I have no ideas how candles are made, and I would rather not go to jail for a course in candle-making, but I'm told that candles are made out of wax, and that wax comes from candles. Now that sounds rather complicated. Like Yin and Yang. Or Verma and Sharma. Or Trumpet and Lumpit.

Anyway, I'll say of this for candles: You can tell when a candle is finishing. You can never tell when the lights are going out.

◆

I learnt to live without light back in the late 1950s, when I rented a couple of rooms in Dehra Dun's Aslley Hall complex. The electricity arrears hadn't been paid for years and stood at an astronomical figure; neither my landlady nor I could clear them. So for two years I went without light. But I had equipped myself with a small kerosene lamp, and it enabled me to sit up late into the night, writing my early stories. Scores of stories were written by lamplight. And sometimes, when there were power cuts and the entire block was plunged into darkness, kids from the neighbouring flats would come over to my place to finish their homework.

There is something very dependable about an oil lamp. Candles burn themselves out, electricity is fickle, but given sufficient oil a lamp will give you company all through the night.

Even a blind man carried a lamp.

'You're blind, why do you carry a lamp?' asked a curious villager.

'So that fools do not stumble against me in the dark,' came the answer.

I did miss my radio, which played on electricity, but around that time the transistor radio was invented, and this could be run on batteries; so I could join the rest of the population in listening to those ball-by-ball cricket commentaries.

In those good old, bad old days, most of our towns did not have proper sanitation, and as late as the 1960s, the top hotels in Mussoorie did not have flush toilets. 'Thunder-boxes' were still the order of the day.

An enterprising young friend devised a portable let seat which could be used independently of a sewage system. He got me to help with a brochure and a name for his invention. We came up with the name 'The Sit Safe'. He was delighted with this and gave me ten rupees—the only time I have received a fee for doing an ad! I hope he made a fortune.

Later, I combined the Boy Scout motto with my name for the toilet seat and devised a motto of my own: 'Be prepared, and sit safe!'

It has served me well over the years.

COME, BLOW YOUR HORN

I am told that India is now the world's third largest producer of motor cars, and I can quite believe it, judging from the volume of traffic and the volume of noise on the road below my window. Indian's burgeoning and prosperous middle-class is on the move, heading for the dizzy heights of Landour and a view of the eternal snows.

Every weekend there is an unending procession of cars going up the hill. This would be wonderful if they were not all blowing their horns at the same time. I had no idea there were so many varieties of motor horn—some hard and clear, some sounding anguished or in deep pain, some imitating the trumpet major in a wedding band, some simply gross... Lying on my bed, hoping for an afternoon nap or an early night's sleep, I am treated to a continuous honking of car horns, and I have learnt to live with it. Sooner or later we can learn to live with anything, especially if we have no choice.

Once upon a time, I would wake to the song of the whistling thrush or mynas squabbling on the windowsill or the jingle of bells as a mule train passed below. Now the whistling thrush comes no more, the mynas have fled, the mule train takes another road. I am woken instead by the rumble of a truck, the roar of a motorcycle revving up, or the blare of car horns greeting the dawn: In the words of the old song, 'Morning Has Broken'. And in more ways than one.

I think Freud would have had something to say about our love affair with the motor horn—the compulsion to play upon it, vigorously, relentlessly, even when the road is clear. I know that pedestrians like me are a nuisance and cyclists no better, but even when we leave the road upon for our speeding friends they will insist on announcing their passing with their hand pressed firmly on the horn.

Talking of speed, it is interesting to know that in the early days of the twentieth century the bicycle was the fastest thing on the road. There was a law that motor vehicle should be preceded by a man carrying a red flag. This law was repealed only when the man with the red flag was knocked over by the vehicle crawling up from behind. Such is progress.

Every year I make one or two trips to Delhi by road. I have always enjoyed this eight-hour drive, especially through the rural areas—the yellow mustard in flower during the winter months, the mango-groves, the sugar cane fields stretching for miles, the winding Ganga canal, even the small wayside towns and villages where roadside dhabas have sprung up, popular with the truck drivers who prefer to drive by night. Modinagar becomes something of a bottleneck, being a sprawling factory town that was mistakenly built beside the road; and as we approach Ghaziabad and Delhi, the road becomes cluttered and hazardous. But it is never dull. There are no dull places in India.

Only once did I fail to enjoy this journey.

I had hired a taxi from Dehra Dun, and the driver was determined to keep his hand on the car horn all the way to Delhi. Even when the road was clear, he had to sound his horn. And to make matters worse, it made a horrible gurgling sound—rather like a buffalo being strangled to death by a boa constrictor. I remonstrated, begged the driver to desist.

'Forgive me, sir, but it's a new horn and I must try it out,' said the driver.

'And what happened to the old one?' I asked.

'It expired,' he said simply. 'Lost its voice.'

Probably from overuse, I thought.

'Well, this one is loud enough,' I said. 'Can't you give it a rest?'

'I want to see if it lasts out until we get to Delhi, sir. Don't you think it has a nice tone?'

'Much too nice,' I said. 'You should donate it to a wedding band.'

When, finally, he deposited me at my destination on the Siri Fort road, I was close to having a nervous breakdown. But my driver was as happy as only a driver with a new horn can be. 'If you need me for the return trip,' he said, 'just give me a ring,' and he gave me his phone number. But for once I took the plane back to Dehra Dun. Planes don't need horns; not yet, anyway. But maybe the day will come when the skies are so overcrowded that planes, like migrating geese, will go honking through the heavens.

Do racing cars come with horns? I wouldn't know, never having been in one. When a Ferrari overtakes a McLaren (or vice versa) does it sound its horn? In the racing world it would be considered impolite, I'm sure. Like a bowler showing a finger to a batsman who has been given out. But then, cricket is no longer a gentleman's game, whereas motor racing appears to engender a spirit of camaraderie, even amongst rivals, probably because the element of risk is shared by all.

Old-fashioned though I am (preferring fish and chips to Hakka noodles), I do my best to keep up-to-date, and roam the TV channels late at night. The other evening, on the BBC I think, we were given a preview of a wonderful new supersonic racing car designed to break the world's speed record. Apparently it can achieve a speed of 1,000MPH. That's faster than sound, I'm told. And being faster than sound, the driver wouldn't hear his own horn since he'd be well ahead of it. Not that it matters. No one is going to get in his way.

Unlike my publisher friend who tried to pick up speed on the Meerut bypass and ran over a pig, killing it instantly; there was a great tamasha, and in the end he had to compensate the owner by paying him twice the value of the pig. My friend insists that he had kept his hand on his car horn all the time, but do pigs, or livestock in general listen to car horns? Stray dogs have learnt to get out of the way. Not having any ownership, they don't merit compensation and must fend for themselves. But pigs, cattle, poultry, donkey and camels don't hear car horns, or pretend not to. They know they are of value to someone, and that a price will be extracted if they come to harm.

Still, better a car with a horn than a car without one. Try getting home from your office with a failed car horn.

And then again, it's one way of expressing yourself. Anger, frustration, despair, or (as in the case of my taxi-driver) just joie de vivre!

THE TROUBLE WITH JINNS

My friend Jimmy has only one arm. He lost the other when he was a young man of twenty-five. The story of how he lost his good right arm is a little difficult to believe, but I swear that it is absolutely true.

To begin with, Jimmy was (and presumably still is) a Jinn. Now a Jinn isn't really a human like us. A Jinn is a spirit creature from another world who has assumed, for a lifetime, the physical aspect of a human being. Jimmy was a true Jinn and he had the Jinn's gift of being able to elongate his arm at will. Most Jinns can stretch their arms to a distance of twenty or thirty feet. Jimmy could attain forty feet. His arm would move through space or up walls or along the ground like a beautiful gliding serpent. I have seen him stretched out beneath a mango tree, helping himself to ripe mangoes from the top of the tree. He loved mangoes. He was a natural glutton and it was probably his gluttony that first led him to misuse his peculiar gifts.

We were at school together at a hill station in northern India. Jimmy was particularly good at basketball. He was clever enough not to lengthen his arm too much because he did not want anyone to know that he was a Jinn. In the boxing ring he generally won his fights. His opponents never seemed to get past his amazing reach. He just kept tapping them on the nose until they retired from the ring bloody and bewildered.

It was during the half-term examinations that I stumbled on Jimmy's secret. We had been set a particularly difficult algebra paper but I had managed to cover a couple of sheets with correct answers and was about to forge ahead on another sheet when I noticed someone's hand on my desk. At first I thought it was the invigilator's. But when I looked up there was no one beside me.

Could it be the boy sitting directly behind? No, he was engrossed in his question paper and had his hands to himself. Meanwhile, the hand on my desk had grasped my answer sheets and was cautiously moving off. Following its descent, I found that it was attached to an arm of amazing length and pliability. This moved stealthily down the desk and slithered across the floor, shrinking all the while, until it was restored to its normal length. Its owner was of course one who had never been any good at algebra.

I had to write out my answers a second time but after the exam I went straight up to Jimmy, told him I didn't like his game and threatened to expose him. He begged me not to let anyone know, assured me that he couldn't really help himself, and offered to be of service to me whenever I wished. It was tempting to have Jimmy as my friend, for with his long reach he would obviously be useful. I agreed to overlook the matter of the pilfered papers and we became the best of pals.

It did not take me long to discover that Jimmy's gift was more of a nuisance than a constructive aid. That was because Jimmy had a second-rate mind and did not know how to make proper use of his powers. He seldom rose above the trivial. He used his long arm in the tuck shop, in the classroom, in the dormitory. And when we were allowed out to the cinema, he used it in the dark of the hall.

Now the trouble with all Jinns is that they have a weakness for women with long black hair. The longer and blacker the hair, the better for Jinns. And should a Jinn manage to take possession of the woman he desires, she goes into a decline and her beauty decays. Everything about her is destroyed except for the beautiful long black hair.

Jimmy was still too young to be able to take possession in this way, but he couldn't resist touching and stroking long black hair. The cinema was the best place for the indulgence of his whims. His arm would start stretching, his fingers would feel their way along the rows of seats, and his lengthening limb would slowly work its way along the aisle until it reached the back of the seat in which sat the object of his admiration. His hand would stroke the long black hair with great tenderness and if the girl felt anything and looked round, Jimmy's hand would disappear behind the seat and lie there poised like the hood of a snake, ready to strike again.

At college, two or three years later, Jimmy's first real victim succumbed to his attentions. She was a lecturer in economics, not very good-looking, but her hair, black and lustrous, reached almost to her knees. She usually kept it in plaits but Jimmy saw her one morning just after she had taken a head bath, and her hair lay spread out on the cot on which she was reclining. Jimmy could no longer control himself. His spirit, the very essence of his personality, entered the woman's body and the next day, she was distraught, feverish and excited. She would not eat, went into a coma, and in a few days, dwindled to a mere skeleton. When she died, she was nothing but skin and bone but her hair had lost none of its loveliness.

I took pains to avoid Jimmy after this tragic event. I could not prove that he was the cause of the lady's sad demise but in my own heart I was quite certain of it. For since meeting

Jimmy, I had read a good deal about Jinns and knew their ways.

We did not see each other for a few years. And then, holidaying in the hills last year, I found we were staying at the same hotel. I could not very well ignore him and after we had drunk a few beers together I began to feel that I had perhaps misjudged Jimmy and that he was not the irresponsible Jinn I had taken him for. Perhaps the college lecturer had died of some mysterious malady that attacks only college lecturers and Jimmy had nothing at all to do with it.

We had decided to take our lunch and a few bottles of beer to a grassy knoll just below the main motor road. It was late afternoon and I had been sleeping off the effects of the beer when I woke upto find Jimmy looking rather agitated.

'What's wrong?' I asked.

'Up there, under the pine trees,' he said. 'Just above the road. Don't you see them?'

'I see two girls,' I said. 'So what?'

'The one on the left. Haven't you noticed her hair?'

'Yes, it is very long and beautiful and—now look, Jimmy, you'd better get a grip on yourself!' But already his hand was out of sight, his arm snaking up the hillside and across the road.

Presently, I saw the hand emerge from some bushes near the girls and then cautiously make its way to the girl with the black tresses. So absorbed was Jimmy in the pursuit of his favourite pastime that he failed to hear the blowing of a horn. Around the bend of the road came a speeding Mercedes Benz truck.

Jimmy saw the truck but there wasn't time for him to shrink his arm back to normal. It lay right across the entire width of the road and when the truck had passed over it, it writhed and twisted like a mortally wounded python.

By the time the truck driver and I could fetch a doctor, the arm (or what was left of it) had shrunk to its ordinary size. We took Jimmy to hospital where the doctors found it necessary to amputate. The truck driver, who kept insisting that the arm he ran over was at least thirty feet long, was arrested on a charge of drunken driving.

Some weeks later, I asked Jimmy, 'Why are you so depressed? You still have one arm. Isn't it gifted in the same way?'

'I never tried to find out,' he said, 'and I'm not going to try now.'

He is, of course, still a Jinn at heart and whenever he sees a girl with long black hair he must be terribly tempted to try out his one good arm and stroke her beautiful tresses. But he has learnt his lesson. It is better to be a human without any gifts than a Jinn or a genius with one too many.

THE POSTMAN KNOCKS

As a freelance writer, most of my adult life has revolved around the coming of the postman. 'A cheque in the mail,' is something that every struggling writer looks forward to. It might, of course, arrive by courier, or it might not come at all. But for the most part, the acceptances and rejections of my writing life, along with editorial correspondence, readers' letters, page proofs and author's copies—how welcome they are!—come through the post.

The postman has always played a very real and important part in my life, and continues to do so. He climbs my twenty-one steps every afternoon, knocks loudly on my door—three raps, so that I know it's him and not some inquisitive tourist—and gives me my registered mail or speed-post with a smile and a bit of local gossip. The gossip is important. I like to know what's happening in the bazaar—who's getting married, who's standing for election, who ran away with the headmaster's wife, and whose funeral procession is passing by. He deserves a bonus for this sort of information.

The courier boy, by contrast, shouts to me from the road below and I have to go down to him. He's mortally afraid of dogs and there are three in the building. My postman isn't bothered by dogs. He comes in all weathers, and he comes on foot except when someone gives him a lift. He turns up when it's snowing, or when it's raining cats and dogs, or when there's a heatwave, and he's quite philosophical about it all. He meets all kinds of people. He has seen joy and sorrow in the homes he visits. He knows something about life. If he wasn't a philosopher to begin with, he will certainly be one by the time he retires.

Of course, not all postmen are paragons of virtue. A few years ago, we had a postman who never got further than the country liquor shop in the bazaar. The mail would pile up there for days, until he sobered up and condescended to deliver it. In due course he was banished to another route, where there were no liquor shops.

We take the postman for granted today, but there was a time, over a hundred years ago, when the carrying of the mails was a hazardous venture, and the mail-runner, or hirkara as he was called, had to be armed with sword or spear. Letters were carried in leather wallets on the backs of runners, who were changed at stages of eight miles. At night, the runners were accompanied by torchbearers—in wilder parts, by drummers called *dug-dugi wallas*—to frighten away wild animals.

The tiger population was considerable at the time, and tigers were a real threat to travellers or anyone who ventured far from their town or village. Mail-runners often fell victim to man-eating tigers. The mail-runners (most of them tribals) were armed with bows and arrows, but these were seldom effective.

In the Hazaribagh district (through which the mail had to be carried, on its way from Calcutta to Allahabad) there appears to have been a concentration of man-eating tigers. There were four passes through this district, and the tigers had them well covered. Williamson, writing in 1810, tells us that the passes were so infested with tigers that the roads were almost impassable.

'Day after day, for nearly a fortnight, some of the dak people were carried off at one or other of these passes.'

In spite of these hazards, a letter sent by dak runner used to take twelve days to reach Meerut from Calcutta. It takes about the same time today, unless you use speed-post.

At upcountry stations the collector of land revenue was the postmaster. He was given a small postal establishment, consisting of a munshi, a matsaddi or sorter, and thirty or forty runners whose pay, in 1804, was five rupees a month. The maintenance of the dak cost the government (i.e., the East India Company) twenty-five rupees a month for each stage of eight miles. Postage stamps were introduced in 1854.

My father was an enthusastic philatelist, and when I was a small boy I would sit and watch him pore over his stamp collection, which included several early and valuable Indian issues. He would grumble at the very dark and smudgy postmarks which obliterated most of Queen Victoria's profile from the stamps. This was due to the composition of the ink used for cancelling the earlier stamps. It was composed of two parts lampblack, four parts linseed oil and three and a half of vinegar.

Letter-distributing peons, or postmen, were always smartly turned out: 'A red turban, a light green chapkan, a small leather belt over the breast and right shoulder, with a chaprass attached showing the peon's number and having the words "Post Office Peon" in English and in two vernaculars, and a bell suspended by a leather strap from the left shoulder.'

Today's postmen are more casual in their attire, although I believe they are still entitled to uniforms. The general public doesn't care how they are dressed, as long as they turn up with those letters containing rakhis or money orders from soldiers, peons and husbands. This is where the postman still scores over the fax and email.

To return to our mail-runners, they were eventually replaced by the dak-ghari, the equivalent of the English 'coach and pair'—which gradually established itself throughout the country.

A survivor into the 1940s, my great-aunt Lillian recalled that in the late nineteenth century, before the coming of the railway, the only way of getting to Dehra Dun was by the dak-*ghari* or Night Mail. Dak-ghari ponies were difficult animals, she told me—'always attempting to turn around and get into the carriage with the passengers!' But once they started there was no stopping them. It was a gallop all the way to the first stage, where the ponies were changed to the accompaniment of a bugle blown by the coachman, in true Dickensian fashion.

The journey through the Siwaliks really began—as it still does—through the Mohand Pass. The ascent starts with a gradual gradient which increases as the road becomes more steep and winding. At this stage of the journey, drums were beaten (if it was day) and torches lit (if it was night) because sometimes wild elephants resented the approach of the dak-*ghari* and, trumpeting a challenge, would throw the ponies into confusion and panic, and send them racing back to the plains.

After 1900, great-aunt Lillian used the train. But the main bus from Saharanpur to Mussoorie still uses the old route through the Siwaliks. And if you are lucky, you may see a herd of wild elephants crossing the road on its way to the Ganga.

And even today, in remote parts of the country, in isolated hill areas where there are no motorable roads, the mail is carried on foot, the postman often covering five or six miles every day. He never runs, true, and might sometimes stop for a glass of tea and a game of cards en route, but he is a reminder of those early pioneers of the postal system, the mail-runners of India.

◆

Let me not cavil at my unexpected visitors. Sometimes they turn out to be very nice people—like the gentleman from Pune who brought me a bottle of whisky and then sat down and drank most of it himself.

LANDOUR BAZAAR

In most North Indian bazaars, there is a clock tower. And like most clocks in clock towers, this one works in fits and starts: listless in summer, sluggish during the monsoon, stopping altogether when it snows in January. Almost every year the tall brick structure gets a coat of paint. It was pink last year. Now it's a livid purple.

From the clock tower at one end to the mule sheds at the other, this old Mussoorie bazaar is a mile long. The tall, shaky three-storey buildings cling to the mountainside, shutting out the sunlight. They are even shakier now that heavy trucks have started rumbling down the narrow street, originally made for nothing heavier than a rickshaw. The street is narrow and damp, retaining all the bazaar smells—sweetmeats frying, smoke from wood or charcoal fires, the sweat and urine of mules, petrol fumes, all these mingle with the smell of mist and old buildings and distant pines.

The bazaar sprang up about 150 years ago to serve the needs of British soldiers who were sent to the Landour convalescent depot to recover from sickness or wounds. The old military hospital, built in 1827, now houses the Defence Institute of

Work Study.* One old resident of the bazaar, a ninety-year-old tailor, can remember the time, in the early years of the century, when the Redcoats marched through the small bazaar on their way to the cantonment church. And they always carried their rifles into church, remembering how many had been surprised in churches during the 1857 uprising.

Today, the Landour bazaar serves the local population, Mussoorie itself being more geared to the needs and interest of tourists. There are a number of silversmiths in Landour. They fashion silver nose rings, earrings, bracelets and anklets, which are bought by the women from the surrounding Jaunpuri villages. One silversmith had a chest full of old silver rupees. These rupees are sometimes hung on thin silver chains and worn as pendants. I have often seen women in Garhwal wearing pendants or necklaces of rupees embossed with the profiles of Queen Victoria or King Edward VII.

At the other extreme there are the kabari shops, where you can pick up almost everything—a tape recorder discarded by a Woodstock student, or a piece of furniture from grandmother's time in the hill station. Old clothes, Victorian bric-a-brac, and bits of modern gadgetry vie for your attention.

The old clothes are often more reliable than the new. Last winter I bought a new pullover marked 'Made in Nepal' from a Tibetan pavement vendor. I was wearing it on the way home when it began to rain. By the time I reached my cottage, the pullover had shrunk inches and I had some difficulty getting out of it! It was now just the right size for Bijju, the milkman's twelve-year-old son, and I gave it to the boy. But it continued to shrink at every wash, and it is now being worn by Teju, Bijju's

---

*The Defence Institute of Work Study has been renamed the Institute of Technologic Management.

younger brother, who is eight.

At the dark windy corner in the bazaar, one always found an old man hunched up over his charcoal fire, roasting peanuts. He'd been there for as long as I could remember, and he could be seen at almost any hour of the day or night, in all weathers.

He was probably quite tall, but I never saw him standing up. One judged his height from his long, loose limbs. He was very thin, probably tubercular, and the high cheekbones added to the tautness of his tightly stretched skin.

His peanuts were always fresh, crisp and hot. They were popular with small boys, who had a few coins to spend on their way to and from school. On cold winter evenings, there was always a demand for peanuts from people of all ages.

No one seemed to know the old man's name. No one had ever thought of asking. One just took his presence for granted. He was as fixed a landmark as the clock tower or the old cherry tree that grew crookedly from the hillside. He seemed less perishable than the tree, more dependable than the clock. He had no family, but in a way all the world was his family because he was in continuous contact with people. And yet he was a remote sort of being; always polite, even to children, but never familiar. He was seldom alone, but he must have been lonely.

Summer nights he rolled himself up in a thin blanket and slept on the ground beside the dying embers of his fire. During winter he waited until the last cinema show was over, before retiring to the rickshaw coolies' shelter where there was protection from the freezing wind.

Did he enjoy being alive? I often wondered. He was not a joyful person; but then neither was he miserable. Perhaps he was one of those who do not attach overmuch importance to themselves, who are emotionally uninvolved in the life around them, content with their limitations, their dark corners; people on whom cares rest lightly, simply because they do not care at all.

I wanted to get to know the old man better, to sound him out on the immense questions involved in roasting peanuts all one's life; but it's too late now. He died last summer.

That corner remained very empty, very dark, and every time I passed it, I was haunted by visions of the old peanut vendor, troubled by the questions I did not ask; and I wondered if he was really as indifferent to life as he appeared to be.

Then, a few weeks ago, there was a new occupant of the corner, a new seller of peanuts. No relative of the old man, but a boy of thirteen or fourteen. The human personality can impose its own nature on its surroundings. In the old man's time it seemed a dark, gloomy corner. Now it's lit up by sunshine—a sunny personality, smiling, chattering. Old age gives way to youth; and I'm glad I won't be alive when the new peanut vendor grows old. One shouldn't see too many people grow old.

Leaving the main bazaar behind, I walk some way down the Mussoorie–Tehri road, a fine road to walk on, in spite of the dust from an occasional bus or jeep. From Mussoorie to Chamba, a distance of some thirty-five miles, the road seldom descends below 7,000 feet, and there is a continual vista of the snow ranges to the north and valleys and rivers to the south. Dhanaulti is one of the lovelier spots, and the Garhwal Mandal Vikas Nigam has a rest house here, where one can spend an idyllic weekend. Some years ago I walked all the way to Chamba, spending the night at Kaddukhal, from where a short climb takes one to the Surkhanda Devi temple.

Leaving the Tehri road, one can also trek down to the little Aglar river and then up to Nag Tibba, 9,000 feet, which has good oak forests and animals ranging from barking deer to Himalayan bear; but this is an arduous trek and you must be prepared to spend the night in the open or seek the hospitality of a village.

On this particular day I reach Suakholi and rest in a tea shop, a loose stone structure with a tin roof held down by stones. It serves the bus passengers, mule drivers, milkmen and others who use this road.

I find a couple of mules tethered to a pine tree. The mule drivers, handsome men in tattered clothes, sit on a bench in the shade of the tree, drinking tea from brass tumblers. The shopkeeper, a man of indeterminate age—the cold dry winds from the mountain passes having crinkled his face like a walnut—greets me enthusiastically, as he always does. He even produces a chair, which looks a survivor from one of Wilson's rest houses, and may even be a Sheraton. Fortunately, the Mussoorie kabaris do not know about it or they'd have snapped it up long ago. In any case, the stuffing has come out of the seat. The shopkeeper apologizes for its condition: 'The rats were nesting in it.' And then, to reassure me: 'But they have gone now.'

I would just as soon be on the bench with the Jaunpuri mule drivers, but I do not wish to offend Mela Ram, the tea shop owner; so I take his chair into the shade and lower myself into it.

'How long have you kept this shop?'

'Oh, ten...fifteen years, I do not remember.' He hasn't bothered to count the years. Why should he? Outside the towns in the isolation of the hills, life is simply a matter of yesterday, today and tomorrow. And not always tomorrow.

Unlike Mela Ram, the mule drivers have somewhere to go and something to deliver—sacks of potatoes! From Jaunpur to Jaunsar, the potato is probably the crop best suited to these stony, terraced fields. They have to deliver their potatoes in the Landour bazaar and return to their villages before nightfall;

and soon they lead their pack animals away, along the dusty road to Mussoorie.

'Tea or lassi?' Mela Ram offers me a choice, and I choose the curd preparation, which is sharp, sour and very refreshing. The wind soughs gently in the upper branches of the pine trees, and I relax in my Sheraton chair like some eighteenth-century nawab who has brought his own furniture into the wilderness. I can see why Wilson did not want to return to the plains when he came this way in the 1850s. Instead, he went further and higher into the mountains and made his home among the people of the Bhagirathi Valley.

Having wandered some way down the Tehri road, it is quite late by the time I return to the Landour bazaar. Lights still twinkle on the hills, but shop fronts are shuttered and the little bazaar is silent. The people living on either side of the narrow street can hear my footsteps, and I hear their casual remarks, music, a burst of laughter.

Through a gap in the rows of buildings I can see Pari Tibba outlined in the moonlight. A greenish phosphorescent glow appears to move here and there about the hillside. This is the 'fairy light' that gives the hill its name Pari Tibba, Fairy Hill. I have no explanation for it, and I don't know anyone else who has been able to explain it satisfactorily; but often from my window I see this greenish light zigzagging about the hill.

A three-quarter moon is up, and the tin roofs of the bazaar, drenched with dew, glisten in the moonlight. Although the street is unlit, I need no torch. I can see every step of the way. I can even read the headlines on the discarded newspaper lying in the gutter.

Although I am alone on the road, I am aware of the life, pulsating around me. It is a cold night, doors and windows are shut; but through the many clinks, narrow fingers of light reach out into the night. Who could still be up? A shopkeeper going through his accounts, a college student preparing for his exams, someone coughing and groaning in the dark.

Three stray dogs are romping in the middle of the road. It is their road now, and they abandon themselves to a wild chase, almost knocking me down.

A jackal slinks across the road, looking to the right and left—he knows his road drill—to make sure the dogs have gone. A field rat wriggles through a hole in a rotting plank on its nightly foray among sacks of grain and pulses.

Yes, this is an old bazaar. The bakers, tailors, silversmiths and wholesale merchants are the grandsons of those who followed the mad Sahibs to this hilltop in the '30s and '40s of the last century. Most of them are plainsmen, quite prosperous, even though many of their houses are crooked and shaky.

Although the shopkeepers and tradesmen are fairly prosperous, the hill people—those who come from the surrounding Tehri and Jaunpur villages—are usually poor. Their small holdings and rocky fields do not provide them with much of a living, and men and boys have to often come into the hill station or go down to the cities in search of a livelihood. They pull rickshaws, or work in hotels and restaurants. Most of them have somewhere to stay.

But as I pass along the deserted street under the shadow of the clock tower, I find a boy huddled in a recess, a thin shawl wrapped around his shoulders. He is wide awake and shivering.

I pass by, my head down, my thoughts already on the warmth of my small cottage only a mile away. And then I stop. It is almost as though the bright moonlight has stopped me, holding my shadow in thrall.

If I am not for myself,

Who will be for me?
And if I am not for others,
What am I?
And if not now, when?

The words of an ancient sage beat upon my mind. I walk back to the shadows where the boy crouches. He does not say anything, but he looks up at me, puzzled and apprehensive. All the warnings of well-wishers crowd in upon me—stories of crime by night, of assault and robbery, 'ill met by moonlight'.

But this is not northern Ireland or Lebanon or the streets of New York. This is Landour in the Garhwal Himalayas. And the boy is no criminal. I can tell from his features that he comes from the hills beyond Tehri. He has come here looking for work and has yet to find any.

'Have you somewhere to stay?' I ask.

He shakes his head; but something about my tone of voice has given him confidence, because now there is a glimmer of hope, a friendly appeal in his eyes.

I have committed myself. I cannot pass on. A shelter for the night—that's the very least one human should be able to expect from another.

'If you can walk some way,' I offer, 'I can give you a bed and blanket.'

He gets up immediately, a thin boy, wearing only a shirt and part of an old tracksuit. He follows me without any hesitation. I cannot now betray his trust. Nor can I fail to trust him.

THE POWER OF PEN AND PAPER

While it is true that I do most of my writing by hand this does not mean that I will use any pencil or pen that comes to hand.

Kind people often give me fountain pens as gifts, unaware that for me the fountain pen is a formidable form of technology, designed with the express purpose of tormenting me. Being one of the clumsiest humans on Earth, I am unable to full or refill or empty a fountain pen of its ink without getting the said ink, black, blue or blue-black, all over my hands or on to my coat-sleeves or shirt front. I will then soil a good handkerchief trying to wipe myself clean. On one occasion, unable to locate a handkerchief, I reached for the nearest piece of cloth, only to realize (too late) that it was a lady's dupatta. That's one way of how to lose friends and fail to influence people.

No, the good old ballpoint is the pen for me. It doesn't make a mess and it can be thrown away when its usefulness is over. There is no bottle of ink waiting to be tipped over on to my writing pad.

Back in my early schooldays we were equipped with pen holders into which nibs had to be inverted. Each student was also given a small inkwell which fitted into a hole in his desk. You had to dip your pen into this little pot of black ink, and then scratch away for a line or two before making another foray into the inkwell. This was a laborious process and often a messy one; but this was how Dickens and Kipling and Tagore and Premchand wrote this novels—dip and scratch, dip and scratch, for days and weeks and months and end. It also meant that you had to take some care of your handwriting, so that the compositor (in the case of an author) or a teacher (in the case of a student) could make out what had been written.

My father used to say that you could judge a man from his handwriting. Mahatma Gandhi had a good, clear hand; so did Abraham Lincoln, Hitler's handwriting deteriorated as time went by, denoting a similar deterioration in his thought processes. But a neat handwriting did not necessarily mean you were a good person. Wainewright, the notorious serial poisoner, had an elegant handwriting; but then, he was also a neat poisoner.

My father wrote a clear, fluent, open script, and he always enjoined on me the importance of good handwriting.

Use large letters, he always told me; write with a bold hand; don't skimp on paper; don't try to squeeze a lot of words into a small space. An open handwriting denotes an open and uncluttered mind. And I think he was right.

Over the years, over these many, many years, I have done most of my writing by hand, only occasionally resorting to a typewriter. As a boy I went to the trouble of taking shorthand and typing lessons; but soon shorthand became obsolete, and now typewriters are obsolete. My great-grandson's laptop looks as though it may also be obsolete very shortly. Fortunately, my writing hand is in good shape, and I can still put down a thousand words before breakfast without any difficulty. If my hand is still in good shape it is probably because it has been wielding a pen or pencil all those years.

♦

'All you need is paper,' said William Saroyan, when asked how one became a writer.

'Paper and pencil will do.'

It was of course a simplification, but there is something about putting pen to paper that is physically as well as mentally satisfying. There is a certain sensuous intimacy about this connection, an intimacy that is absent from any other form of writing. Maybe it's the texture and touch of the paper, the flow of ink, the movement of the pen, the connection of all three with the human hand and the hand's connection with the mind of the writer.

It all amounts to the power of the pen.

◆

Mark Twain tried an experiment to see if he could convey his thoughts to someone simply by putting them down on paper—and leaving them there.

He wrote a long letter to a friend but instead of posting it he crumpled it up and dropped it in his wastepaper basket. A week later, he met his friend who told him that he had been constantly thinking of the writer and that he had been aware of Mark Twain's own thoughts and feelings, almost as though they had been communicated through some intangible means.

Mark Twain then wrote a letter to one of his publishers, complaining of a delay in royalty payments. He did not post the letter. But a few days later he received his royalties!

Fellow writes who have issues with their publisher can try this method of obtaining satisfaction. However, I give no guarantee that it will work.

WELCOME, GOOD SPIRITS!

The British left India in 1947, but they left their ghosts behind. In old dak bungalows across the country, in forest rest houses, in hill stations, in cantonment towns and seaside resorts, the traveller might well encounter the resident spirit of a former sahib or memsahib determined to 'stay on, in spirit if not in the flesh'.

I live in Landour, the cantonment area just above Mussoorie, and most of the houses on the hillside were built well over a hundred years ago. In fact, some of them go back to the founding of this hill station in the 1820s. The old cemetery, facing the eternal snows, provided shelter to the graves of the many soldiers and officers who were brought to this convalescent depot, in order to recuperate from wounds or illnesses. Not everyone recovered. Families came up too, to get away from the heat and dust of the plains, but infant mortality was high, even in hill stations. The graves of mothers and small children dot the hillside.

You are unlikely to encounter a ghost during a walk past the cemetery, but some of the old houses are reputed to be haunted. Not so long ago, on an early morning walk, I met a family from Delhi hurriedly vacating a guest house, complaining that they had been kept up all night by the visitations of a weeping lady who was wandering about in search of a lost child. Afraid that she might make off with one of their children, they quit the place in a hurry.

I live in a very old house, and although I am not prone to seeing ghosts, I do hear them occasionally.

Late at night, I hear desultory conversations taking place in the sitting room which adjoins my bedroom. No one sleeps there. Rakesh and Beena have their room at the other end of the flat. But the conversations go on for some time, becoming quite lively as the night progresses. I can't make out what is being said, but a party appears to be in progress, perhaps a Christmas party from long long ago, their talk and laughter trapped in the warp of time.

One night, feeling hungry myself, I got up and went into the front room, switching on all the lights. There was no one there. When I returned to my room, the party began again! It must have been a very exclusive party, if they didn't want me butting in.

But they must have relented and felt sorry for me. This morning, as I opened my doors to the early December sunshine, I found a large Christmas plum pudding on the table in my front room. There was no card or note beside it. How did it get there and that too with all the doors closed? Did my spooky late night visitants leave it there for me? I decided to taste some of it—just in case it was over a hundred years old.

Well, it's a perfectly good pudding. Just the right amount of brandy in it. I think I'll have another slice. And if my ghostly partygoers are here again tonight, I won't complain.

THE INDIA I CARRIED WITH ME

A m now going back in time, to a period when I was caught between East and West, and had to make up my mind just where I belonged. I had been away from India for barely a month before I was longing to return. The insularity of the place where I found myself (Jersey, in the Channel Islands) had something to do with it, I suppose. There was little there to remind me of India or the East, not one brown face to be seen in the streets or on the beaches. I'm sure it's a different sort of place now; but fifty years ago it had nothing to offer by way of companionship or good cheer to a lonely, sensitive boy who had left home and friends in search of a 'better future'.

I had come to England with a dream of sorts, and I was to return to India with another kind of dream; but in between there were to be four years of dreary office work, lonely bed-sitting rooms, shabby lodging houses, cheap snack bars, hospital wards, and the struggle to write my first book and find a publisher for it.

I started work in a large departmental store called *Le Riche*. At eight in the morning, when I walked to the store, it was dark. At six in the evening, when I walked home, it was dark again. Where were all those sunny beaches Jersey was famous for? I would have to wait for summer to see them, and a

Saturday afternoon to take a dip in the sea.

Occasionally, after an early supper, I would walk along the deserted seafront. If the tide was in and the wind approaching gale-force, the waves would climb the sea wall and drench me with their cold salt spray. My aunt, with whom I was staying, thought I was quite mad to take this solitary walk; but I have always been at one with nature, even in its wilder moments, and the wind and the crashing waves gave me a sense of freedom, strengthened my determination to escape from the island and go my own way.

When I wasn't walking along the seafront, I would sit at the portable typewriter in my small attic room, and hammer out the rough chapters of the book that was to become my first novel. These were characters and incidents based on the journal I had kept during my last year in India. It was 1951, recalled in late 1952. An eighteen-year-old looking back on incidents in the life of a seventeen-year-old! Nostalgia and longing suffused those pages. How I longed to be back with my friends in the small town of Dehra Dun—a leafy place, sunny, fruit-laden, easy—going every familiar corner etched clearly in my memory. Somehow, it had been that last year in Dehra that had brought me closer to the India that I had so far only taken for granted. An India of close and sometimes sentimental friendships. Of striking contrasts: a small cinema showing English pictures (a George Formby comedy or an American musical) and only a couple of hours away thousands taking a dip in the sacred water of the Ganga. Or outside the station, hundreds of pony-drawn tongas waiting to pick up passengers, while the more affluent climbed into their Ford Convertibles, Morris Minors, Baby Austins or flashy Packards and Daimlers.

But of course Dehra in the 'fifties' was a town of bicycles.

Students, shopkeepers, Army cadets, office workers, all used them. The scooter (or Lambretta) had only just been invented, and it would be several years before it took over from the bicycle. It was still unaffordable for the great majority.

I was awkward on a bicycle and frequently fell off, breaking my arm on one occasion. But this did not prevent me from joining my friends on cycle rides to the Sulphur springs, or to Premnagar (where the Military Academy was situated) or along the Haridwar road and down to the riverbed at Lachiwala.

In Jersey, I found an old cycle belonging to my cousin, and I rode from St. Helier where we lived, to St. Brelade's Bay, at the other end of the island. But returning after dark, I was hauled up for riding without lights. I had no idea that cycles had also to be equipped with lights. Back in Dehra, we never used them!

The attic room had no view, so one of my favourite occupations, gazing out of windows, came to a stop. But perhaps this was helpful in that it made me concentrate on the sheet of paper in my typewriter. After about six months, I had a book of sorts ready for submission to any publisher who was prepared to look at it. Meanwhile, I had been through at least three jobs and had even been offered a post in the Jersey Civil Service, having successfully taken the local civil service exam—something I had done out of sheer boredom, as I had no intention of settling permanently on the island.

I had been keeping a diary of sorts and in some of the entries I had expressed my desire to get back to India, and my discontent at having to stay with relatives who were unsympathetic, not only to my feelings for India but also to my ambitions to become a writer. The diary fell into my uncle's hands. He read it, and was naturally upset. We had a row. I was contrite; but a few days later I packed my suitcases (all two of them) and stepped on to the ferry that was to take me to Southampton and then to London. Lesson one: don't leave your personal diaries lying around!

But perhaps it was all for the best, otherwise I might have hung around in Jersey for another year or two, to the detriment of my personal happiness and my writing ambitions.

I arrived in London in the middle of a thick yellow November fog—those were the days of the killer London fogs—and after a search found the Students' Hostel where I was given a cubicle to myself. But I did not stay there very long; the available food was awful. As soon as I got an office job—not too difficult in the 1950s—I rented an attic room in Belsize Park, the first of many bedsitters that I was to live in during my three-year sojourn in London.

From Belsize Park I was to move to Haverstock Hill (close to Hampstead Heath), then to South London for a short time, and finally to Swiss Cottage. Most of my landladies were Jewish—refugees from persecution in pre-war Europe—and I too was a refugee of sorts, still very unsure of where I belonged. Was it England, the land of my father, or India, the land of my birth? But my father had also been born in India, had grown up and made a living there, visiting *his* father's land, England, only a couple of times during his life.

The link with Britain was tenuous, based on heredity rather than upbringing. It was more in the mind. It was a literary England I had been drawn to, not a physical England. And in fact, I took several exploratory walks around 'literary' London, visiting houses or streets where famous writers had once lived; in particular the East End and Dockland, for I had grown up on the novels and stories of Dickens, Smollett, Captain Marryat, and W.W. Jacobs. But I did not make many English friends. If they were a reserved race, I was even more reserved. Always shy, I waited for others to take the initiative. In India, people will take the initiative, they lose no time in getting to know you. Not so in England. They were too polite to look at you. And in that respect, I was more English than the English.

The gentleman who lived on the floor below me occasionally went so far as to greet me with the observation, 'Beastly weather, isn't it?'

And I would respond by saying, 'Oh, perfectly beastly,' and pass on.

How different it was when I bumped into a Gujarati boy, Praveen, who lived on the basement floor. He gave me a winning smile, and I remember saying, 'Oh, to be in Bombay now that winter's here,' and immediately we were friends.

He was only seventeen, a year or two younger than me, and he was studying at one of the polytechnics with a view to getting into the London School of Economics. At that time, most of the Indians in London were students, the great immigration rush was still a long way off, and racial antagonisms were directed more at the recently arrived West Indians than at Asians.

Praveen took me on the rounds of the coffee bars, then proliferating all over London, and introduced me to other students, among them a Vietnamese, called Thanh, who cultivated my friendship because, as he said, 'I want to speak English.' When he discovered that my accent was very un-English (you could have called it Welsh with an Anglo-Indian interaction), he dropped me like a hot brick. He was very frank, he was not interested in friendship, he said, only in improving his accent. I heard later that he'd attached himself to a young journalist from up north, who spoke broad Yorkshire.

Most evenings I remained in my room and worked on my novel. From being a journal it had become a first person narrative, and now I was turning it into fiction in the third person. The title had also undergone a few changes, but finally, I settled on *The Room on the Roof.*

Into it, I put all the love and affection I felt for the friends I had left behind in Dehra. It was more than nostalgia, it was a recreation of the people, places and incidents of that last year in India. I did not want it to fade away. The riverbanks at Haridwar, the mango-groves of the Doon, the poinsettias and bougainvillaea, the games on the parade ground, the chaat shops near the Clock Tower, the summer heat, the monsoon downpours, romping naked in the rain, sitting on railway platforms, gnawing at a stick of sugar cane, listening to street cries... All this and more came crowding upon me as I sat writing before the gas fire in my little room.

When it grew very cold, I used an old overcoat given to me by Diana Athill, the junior partner at Andre Deutsch, who had promised to publish *The Room...* if I rewrote it as a novel. Another who encouraged me was a BBC producer, Prudence Smith, who got me to give a couple of talks on Radio's Third Programme. I felt I was getting somewhere; and when I found myself confined to the Hampstead General Hospital for almost a month, with a mysterious disease which had affected the vision in my right eye, I used the left to catch up on my reading and to write a couple of short stories.

A nurse brought a tray of books around the ward every afternoon, and thanks to this courtesy, I was able to discover the delightful stories of William Saroyan and Denton Welch's sensitive first novel *Maiden Voyage.* Saroyan, a Pulitzer Prize winner for his play *The Time of Your Life,* was then very successful and popular. Denton's promising career had been cut short by a terrible accident. Out cycling on a country road, he had been knocked down by a speeding motorist.

He had lived for several years, struggling against crippling injuries and almost completing his sensitive autobiography *A Voice in the Clouds*. He was thirty- one when he died. Towards the end, he could only work for three or four minutes at a time. Complications set in, and the left side of his heart started failing. Even then he made a terrific effort to finish his book. His friend Eric wrote—'Denton was upheld by the high courage which seemed somehow the fruit of his rare intelligence.'

The work of these writers, together with the bottle of Guinness I was given every day as a tonic (they had found me somewhat undernourished), meant that I walked out of the hospital with a spring in my step and a determination to succeed.

But Andre Deutsch was still dithering over my book. The firm was doing well, but he didn't like taking risks. No publisher likes losing money. And he wasn't going to make much out of my novel, a subjective and unsensational work.

But I resented his indecision. So I returned the small amount he'd paid me by way of an option, and demanded the return of my manuscript. Back came an apologetic letter and an advance (then £50) against publication.

Today, almost fifty years later, the firm of Andre Deutsch has gone, but *The Room on the Roof* is still in print, still making friends. This is not something that I gloat over, it only goes to show that books are unpredictable commodities, and that the most successful authors and publishers often fall by the wayside. Publishers go out of business, writers fade from the public mind. Even Saroyan is forgotten now. I'll be forgotten too, someday.

There were to be further delays before The *Room...* was published, and I was back in India when it did come out. By then I'd almost forgotten about the book! But it picked up the John Llewellyn Rhys Prize, an award that also went to V.S. Naipaul a year later, for his first book. It was then worth only £50. There were no big sponsors in those days. It is now sponsored by a British newspaper and is worth £5,000. This was turned down last year by another Indian writer, who disagreed with the paper's policies.

Meanwhile, in London, there were other distractions. I loved stage musicals, and if I had a little money to spare I went to the theatre, taking in such productions as *Porgy and Bess, Paint Your Wagon, Pal Joey, Teahouse of the August Moon,* and the occasional review. And of course the annual presentation of *Peter Pan* at the Scala theatre, not far from where I worked. I had grown up on Peter Pan, first read to me by my father in distant Jamnagar, and at school I had read Barrie's other plays and been charmed by them; but, like operetta, they had gone out of fashion and only the ageless Peter remained. 'Do you believe in fairies?' he asks in the play. And to save Tinker Bell from extinction, I clapped with the rest of the audience. But did I really believe in fairies? I looked for them in Kensington Gardens, where Peter Pan's statue stood, and found a few mothers pushing their perambulators, but no fairies. And I looked in Hyde Park, but found only courting couples. And I looked all over Leicester Square, but instead of fairies I found prostitutes soliciting business. As I was still looking for romance, I crept back to my room and my portable typewriter—I would have to create my own romance.

The small portable had been in the windows of a Jersey department store, and every time I passed the store I glanced at the window to see if the typewriter was still there. It seemed to be waiting for me to come in and take it away. I longed to buy it, partly because I had to type out the final drafts of my book, and also because it looked very dainty and attractive. It was definitely out to seduce me. Finally, with the help of a loan from Mr Bromley, a kindly senior clerk, I bought the machine. It cost only £12, but that was three month's wages at the time. It accompanied me to London, and then a couple of years later to India, giving me good service in Dehra Dun, New Delhi, and then Mussoorie where it finally succumbed to the damp monsoon climate.

My worldly possessions had increased, not only by the typewriter, but also by a record player which I had bought second-hand from a Thai student. I had become an ardent fan of the black singer, Eartha Kitt, and had bought all her records; but they were no good without a player until the Thai boy came to my rescue. Then the sensual, throaty voice of Eartha reverberated through the lodging house, bringing complaints from the landlady and the gentleman downstairs. I had to keep the volume low, which wasn't much fun.

I was also fond of the clarinet (turj) playing of an Indian musician, Master Ibrahim, and I had some of his recordings which transported me back to the streets and bazaars of small-town India. Light, lilting and tuneful, I preferred this sort of flute music to the warblings of the more popular songsters.

Praveen liked gangster films and wanted me to accompany him to anything which featured Humphrey Bogart, James Cagney, George Raft and other tough guys. Praveen wanted to be a tough guy himself and often struck a Bogart-like pose, cigarette dangling from the side of his mouth. There was nothing tough about Praveen, who was really rather delicate, but his affectations were charming and risible.

One day he announced that he was returning to India for a few months, as his ailing mother was anxious to see him. He asked me to come along too, to give him company during the three-week voyage. To do so, I would have to throw up my job, but I had already thrown up several jobs. They were simply stopgaps until I could establish myself as a writer. I hadn't the slightest intention or ambition of being a senior clerk or even an executive for the firm in which I was working. The only problem in leaving England then was that I would have to leave my book in limbo, as there was still no guarantee that Deutsch would publish it. But it was time I went on to write other things; time to strike out on my own, to take a chance with India. The ships were full of British and Anglo-Indian families coming to England, to make a 'better future' for themselves. I would do the opposite, go into reverse, and make my future, for good or ill, in the land of my birth.

My passport was in order, and I had only to give a week's notice to my employers. I had saved up about £200, and of this £50 went on the cost of my passage, London to Bombay. Praveen and I boarded the S.S. *Balory,* a Polish liner with a reputation for running into trouble. We had no difficulty in securing berths in tourist class. Praveen had every intention of returning to England to complete his studies. My own intentions were very vague. I knew there would be no job for me in India, but I was quietly confident that I could make a living from writing, and that too in the English language.

The *Balory* lived up to its reputation. Some of the crew went missing at Gibraltar. A passenger fell overboard in the Red Sea. Lifeboats were lowered, but he could not be found.

Praveen fell in love with an Egyptian girl who disembarked at Aden. He followed her ashore, and I had to run after him and get him back to the ship. As we docked at Ballard Pier, a fire broke out in one of the holds, but by then, we were safely ashore. Praveen was swamped by relatives who carried him off to the suburbs of Bombay. I made my way to Victoria

Terminus and boarded the Dehra Dun Express. It was a slow passenger train, which went chugging through several states in the general direction of northern India. Two days and two nights later we crawled through the eastern Doon. It was early March. The mango trees were in blossom, the peacocks were calling, and Belsize Park was far away.

THE MAN WHO WAS KIPLING

I was sitting on a bench in the Indian Section of the Victoria and Albert Museum in London, when a tall, stooping, elderly gentleman sat down beside me. I gave him a quick glance, noting his swarthy features, heavy moustache and horn-rimmed spectacles. There was something familiar and disturbing about his face, and I couldn't resist looking at him again.

I noticed that he was smiling at me.

'Do you recognize me?' he asked, in a soft pleasant voice.

'Well, you do seem familiar,' I said. 'Haven't we met somewhere?'

'Perhaps. But if I seem familiar to you, that is at least something. The trouble these days is that people don't *know* me anymore—I'm a familiar, that's all. Just a name standing for a lot of outmoded ideas.'

A little perplexed, I asked, 'What is it you do?'

'I wrote books once. Poems and tales... Tell me, whose books do you read?'

'Oh, Maugham, Priestley, Thurber. And among the older lot, Bennett and Wells—.' I hesitated, groping for an important name, and I noticed a shadow, a sad shadow, pass across my companion's face.

'Oh, yes, and Kipling,' I said. 'I read a lot of Kipling.'

His face brightened up at once, and the eyes behind the thick-lensed spectacles suddenly came to life.

'I'm Kipling,' he said.

I stared at him in astonishment, and then, realizing that he might perhaps be dangerous, I smiled feebly and said, 'Oh, yes?'

'You probably don't believe me. I'm dead, of course.'

'So I thought.'

'And you don't believe in ghosts?'

'Not as a rule.'

'But you'd have no objection to talking to one, if he came along?'

'I'd have no objection. But how do I know you're Kipling? How do I know you're not an imposter?'

'Listen, then:

When my heavens were turned to blood,
When the dark had filled my day,
Furthest, but most faithful, stood
That lone star I cast away.
I had loved myself, and I
Have not lived and dare not die.'

'Once,' he said, gripping me by the arm and looking me straight in the eye. 'Once in life I watched a star; but I whistled her to go.'

'Your star hasn't fallen yet,' I said, suddenly moved, suddenly quite certain that I sat beside Kipling. 'One day, when there is a new spirit of adventure abroad, we will discover you again.'

'Why have they heaped scorn on me for so long?'

'You were too militant, I suppose—too much of an Empire man. You were too patriotic for your own good.'

He looked a little hurt. 'I was never very political,' he said. 'I wrote over six hundred poems, and you could only call a dozen of them political, I have been abused for harping on the theme of the White Man's Burden but my only aim was to show off the Empire to my audience—and I believed the Empire was a fine and noble thing. Is it wrong to believe in something? I never went deeply into political issues, that's true. You must remember, my seven years in India were very youthful years. I was in my twenties, a little immature if you like, and my interest in India was a boy's interest. Action appealed to me more than anything else. You must understand that.'

'No one has described action more vividly, or India so well. I feel at one with Kim wherever he goes along the Grand Trunk Road, in the temples at Banaras, amongst the Saharanpur fruit gardens, on the snow-covered Himalayas. Kim has colour and movement and poetry.'

He sighed, and a wistful look came into his eyes.

'I'm prejudiced, of course,' I continued. 'I've spent most of my life in India—not *your* India, but an India that does still have much of the colour and atmosphere that you captured. You know, Mr Kipling, you can still sit in a third-class railway carriage and meet the most wonderful assortment of people. In any village you will still find the same courtesy, dignity and courage that the Lama and Kim found on their travels.'

'And the Grand Trunk Road? Is it still a long winding procession of humanity?'

'Well, not exactly,' I said, a little ruefully. 'It's just a procession of motor vehicles now. The poor Lama would be run down by a truck if he became too dreamy on the Grand Trunk Road. Times *have* changed. There are no more Mrs Hawksbees in Simla, for instance.'

There was a faraway look in Kipling's eyes. Perhaps he was imagining himself a boy again; perhaps he could see the hills or the red dust of Rajputana; perhaps he was having a private conversation with Privates Mulvaney and Ortheris, or perhaps he was out hunting with the Seonce wolf pack. The sound of London's traffic came to us through the glass doors, but we heard only the creaking of bullock-cart wheels and the distant music of a flute.

He was talking to himself, repeating a passage from one of his stories. 'And the last puff of the day wind brought from the unseen villages the scent of damp woodsmoke, hot cakes, dripping undergrowth, and rotting pine cones. That is the true smell of the Himalayas, and if once it creeps into the blood of a man, that man will at the last, forgetting all else, return to the hills to die.'

A mist seemed to have risen between us—or had it come in from the streets?—and when it cleared, Kipling had gone away.

I asked the gatekeeper if he had seen a tall man with a slight stoop, wearing spectacles.

'Nope,' said the gatekeeper. 'Nobody been by for the last ten minutes.'

'Did someone like that come into the gallery a little while ago?'

'No one that I recall. What did you say the bloke's name was?'

'Kipling,' I said.

'Don't know him.'

'Didn't you ever read *The Jungle Book*?'

'Sounds familiar. Tarzan stuff, wasn't it?'

I left the museum, and wandered about the streets for a long time, but I couldn't find Kipling anywhere. Was it the boom of London's traffic that I heard, or the boom of the Sutlej river racing through the valleys?

CALYPSO CHRISTMAS

My first Christmas in London had been a lonely one. My small bed-sitting room near Swiss Cottage had been cold and austere, and my landlady had disapproved of any sort of revelry. Moreover, I hadn't the money for the theatre or a good restaurant. That first English Christmas was spent sitting in front of a lukewarm gas fire, eating beans on toast, and drinking cheap sherry. My one consolation was the row of Christmas cards on the mantelpiece—most of them from friends in India.

But in the following year I was making more money and living in a bigger, brighter, homelier room. The new landlady approved of my bringing friends—even girls—to the house, and had even made me a plum pudding so that I could entertain my guests. My friends in London included a number of Indian and Commonwealth students, and through them I met George, a friendly, sensitive person from Trinidad.

George was not a student. He was over thirty. Like thousands of other West Indians, he had come to England because he had been told that jobs were plentiful, that there was a free health scheme and national insurance, and that he could earn anything from ten to twenty pounds a week—far more than he could make in Trinidad or Jamaica. But, while it was true that jobs were to be had in England, it was also true that sections of local labour resented outsiders filling these posts. There were also those, belonging chiefly to the lower middle-classes, who were prone to various prejudices, and though these people were a minority, they were still capable of making themselves felt and heard.

In any case, London is a lonely place, especially for the stranger. And for the happy-go-lucky West Indian, accustomed to sunshine, colour and music, London must be quite baffling.

As though to match the grey-green fogs of winter, Londoners wore sombre colours, greys and browns. The West Indians couldn't understand this. Surely, they reasoned, during a grey season the colours worn should be vivid reds and greens— colours that would defy the curling fog and uncomfortable rain? But Londoners frowned on these gay splashes of colour: to them it all seemed an expression of some sort of barbarism. And then again, Londoners had a horror of any sort of loud noise, and a blaring radio could (quite justifiably) bring in scores of protests from neighbouring houses. The West Indians, on the other hand, liked letting off steam; they liked holding parties in their rooms at which there was much singing and shouting. They had always believed that England was their mother country, and so, despite rain, fog, sleet and snow, they were determined to live as they had lived back home in Trinidad. And it is to their credit, and even to the credit of indigenous Londoners, that this is what they succeeded in doing.

George worked for the British Railways. He was a ticket collector at one of the underground stations; he liked his work, and received about ten pounds a week for collecting tickets. A large, stout man, with huge hands and feet, he always had a gentle, kindly expression on his mobile face. Amongst other accomplishments he could play the piano, and as there was an old, rather dilapidated piano in my room, he would often come over in the evenings to run his fat, heavy fingers over the keys, playing tunes that ranged from hymns to jazz pieces. I thought he would be a nice person to spend Christmas with, so I asked him to come and share the pudding my landlady had made, and a bottle of sherry I had procured.

Little did I realize that an invitation to George would he interpreted as an invitation to all of George's friends and relations—in fact, anyone who had known him in Trinidad—but this was the way he looked at it, and at eight o' clock on Christmas Eve, while a chilly wind blew dead leaves down from Hampstead Heath, I saw a veritable army of West Indians marching down Belsize Avenue, with George in the lead.

Bewildered, I opened my door to them; and in streamed George, George's cousins, George's nephews and George's friends. They were all smiling and shaking hands with me, making complimentary remarks about my room ('Man, that's some piano!' 'Hey, look at that crazy picture!' 'This rocking chair gives me fever!') and took no time at all to feel and make themselves at home. Everyone had brought something along for the party. George had brought several bottles of beer. Eric, a flashy, coffee-coloured youth, had brought cigarettes and more beer. Marian, a buxom woman of thirty-five, who called me 'darling' as soon as we met, and kissed me on the cheeks saying she adored pink cheeks, had brought bacon and eggs. Her daughter Lucy, who was sixteen and in the full bloom of youth, had brought a gramophone, while the little nephews carried the records. Other friends and familiars had also brought beer; and one enterprising fellow produced a bottle of Jamaican rum.

Then everything began to happen at once.

Lucy put a record on the gramophone, and the strains of 'Basin Street Blues' filled the room. At the same time George sat down at the piano to hammer out an accompaniment to the record: his huge hands crushed down on the keys as though he were chopping up chunks of meat. Marian had lit the gas fire and was busy frying bacon and eggs. Eric was opening beer bottles. In the midst of the noise and confusion I heard a knock on the door—a very timid, hesitant sort of knock—and opening it, found my landlady standing on the threshold.

'Oh, Mr Bond, the neighbours—' she began; and glancing into the room was rendered speechless.

'It's only tonight,' I said. 'They'll all go home after an hour. Remember, it's Christmas!'

She nodded mutely and hurried away down the corridor, pursued by something called 'Be-Bop-A-Lola'. I closed the door and drew all the curtains in an effort to stifle the noise; but everyone was stamping about on the floorboards, and I hoped fervently that the downstairs people had gone to the theatre. George had started playing calypso music, and Eric and Lucy were strutting and stomping in the middle of the room, while the two nephews were improvising on their own. Before I knew what was happening, Marian had taken me in her strong arms, and was teaching me to do the calypso. The song playing, I think, was 'Banana Boat Song'.

Instead of the party lasting an hour, it lasted three hours. We ate innumerable fried eggs and finished off all the beer. I took turns dancing with Marian, Lucy and the nephews. There was a peculiar expression they used when excited. 'Fire!' they shouted. I never knew what was supposed to be on fire, or what the exclamation implied, but I too shouted 'Fire!' and somehow it seemed a very sensible thing to shout.

Perhaps their hearts were on fire, I don't know; but for all their excitability and flashiness and brashness they were lovable and sincere friends, and today, when I look back on my two years in London, that Christmas party is the brightest, most vivid memory of all, and the faces of George and Marian, Lucy and Eric, are the faces I remember best.

At midnight someone turned out the light. I was dancing with Lucy at the time, and in the dark she threw her arms around me and kissed me full on the lips. It was the first time I had been kissed by a girl, and when I think about it, I am glad that it was Lucy who kissed me.

When they left, they went in a bunch, just as they had come. I stood at the gate and watched them saunter down the dark, empty street. The buses and tubes had stopped running at midnight, and George and his friends would have to walk all the way back to their rooms at Highgate and Golders Green.

After they had gone, the street was suddenly empty and silent, and my own footsteps were the only sounds I could hear. The cold came clutching at me, and I turned up my collar. I looked up at the windows of my house, and at the windows of all the other houses in the street. They were all in darkness. It seemed to me that we were the only ones who had really celebrated Christmas.

UP AT SISTERS BAZAAR

A few years ago I spent a couple of summers up at Sisters Bazaar, at the farthest extremity of Mussoorie's Landour cantonment—an area as yet untouched by the tentacles of a bulging, disoriented octopus of a hill station.

There were a number of residences up at Sisters, most of them old houses, but they were at some distance from each other, separated by clumps of oak or stands of deodar. After sundown, flying foxes swooped across the roads, and the nightjar set up its nocturnal chant. Here, I thought, I would live like Thoreau at Walden Pond—alone, aloof, far from the strife and cacophony of the vast amusement park that was now Mussoorie. How wrong I was proved to be!

To begin with, I found that almost everyone on the hillside was busily engaged in writing a book. Was the atmosphere really so conducive to creative activity, or was it just a conspiracy to put me out of business? The discovery certainly put me out of my stride completely, and it was several weeks before I could write a word.

There was a retired Brigadier who was writing a novel about World War II, and a retired Vice Admiral who was writing a book about a Rear Admiral. Mrs S, who had been an actress in the early days of the talkies, was writing poems in the manner of

Wordsworth; and an ageing (or rather, resurrected) ex-Maharani was penning her memoirs. There was also an elderly American who wrote salacious bestselling novels about India. It was said of him that he looked like Hemingway and wrote like Charles Bronson.

With all this frenzied literary activity going on around me, it wasn't surprising that I went into shock for some time.

I was saved (or so I thought) by a 'far-out' ex-hippie and ex-Hollywood scriptwriter who decided he would produce a children's film based on one of my stories. It was a pleasant little story, and all would have gone well if our producer friend hadn't returned from some high-altitude poppy fields in a bit of a trance and failed to notice that his leading lady was in the family way. Although the events of the story all took place in a single day, the film itself took about four months to complete, with the result that her figure altered considerably from scene to scene until, by late evening of the same day, she was displaying all the glories of imminent motherhood.

Naturally, the film was never released. I believe our producer friend now runs a health-food restaurant in Sydney. I shared a large building (it had paper-thin walls) with several other tenants, one of whom, a French girl in her thirties, was learning to play the sitar. She and her tabla-playing companion would sleep by day, but practise all through the night, making sleep impossible for me or anyone else in my household. I would try singing operatic arias to drown her out, but you can't sing all night and she always outlasted me. Even a raging forest fire, which forced everyone else to evacuate the building for a night, did not keep her from her sitar any more than Rome burning kept Nero from his fiddle. Finally I got one of the chowkidar's children to pour sand into her instrument, and that silenced her for some time.

Another tenant who was there for a short while was a

Dutchman, (yes, we were a cosmopolitan lot in the 1980s, before visa regulations were tightened) who claimed to be an acupuncturist. He showed me his box of needles and promised to cure me of the headaches that bothered me from time to time. But before he could start the treatment, he took a tumble while coming home from a late night party and fell down the khud into a clump of cacti, the sharp pointed kind, which punctured the more tender parts of his anatomy. He had to spend a couple of weeks in the local mission hospital, receiving more conventional treatment, and he never did return to cure my headaches.

How did Sisters Bazaar come by its name?

Well, in the bad old, good old days, when Landour was a convalescent station for sick and weary British soldiers, the nursing sisters had their barracks in the long, low building that lines the road opposite Prakash's Store. On the old maps this building is called The Sisters. For a time it belonged to Dev Anand's family, but I believe it has since changed hands.

Of a 'bazaar' there is little evidence, although Prakash's Store must be at least a hundred years old. It is famous for its home-made cheese, and tradition has it that several generations of the Nehru family have patronized the store, from Motilal Nehru in the 1920s, to Rahul and his mother in more recent times.

I am more of a jam-fancier myself, and although I no longer live in the area, I do sometimes drop into the store for a can of raspberry or apricot or plum jam, made from the fruit brought here from the surrounding villages.

Further down the road is Dahlia Bank, where dahlias once covered the precipitous slope (known as the 'Eyebrow'), behind the house. The old military hospital (which was opened in 1827), has been altered and expanded to house the present Defence

Institute of Work Study. Beyond it lies Mount Hermon, with the lonely grave of a lady who perished here one wild and windy winter, 150 years ago. And close by lies the lovely Oakville Estate, where at least three generations of the multitalented Alter fancily have lived. They do everything from acting in Hindi films to climbing greasy poles, Malkhumb-style. From wise old Bob to Steve and Andy, those Alter boys are mighty handy.

It is cold up there in winter, and I now live about 500 feet lower down, where it is only slightly warmer. But my walks take me up the hill from time to time. Most of the unusual eccentric people I have written about have gone away, but others, equally interesting, have taken their place. But for news of them you'll have to wait for my autobiography. The Mussoorie gossips will then get a dose of their own medicine. Let them start having sleepless nights.

WHISPERING IN THE DARK

A wild night. Wind moaning, trees lashing themselves in a frenzy, rain beating down on the road, thunder over the mountains. Loneliness stretched ahead of me, a loneliness of the heart as well as a physical loneliness. The world was blotted out by a mist that had come up from the valley; a thick, white, clammy shroud.

I groped through the forest, groped in my mind for the memory of a mountain path, some remembered rock or ancient deodar. Then a streak of blue lightning gave me a glimpse of a barren hillside and a house cradled in mist.

It was an old-world house, built of limestone rock on the outskirts of a crumbling hill station. There was no light in its windows; probably the electricity had been disconnected long ago. But if I could get in it would do for the night.

I had no torch, but at times the moon shone through the wild clouds, and trees loomed out of the mist like primeval giants. I reached the front door and found it locked from within. I walked round to the side and broke a windowpane, put my hand through shattered glass and found the bolt.

The window, warped by over a hundred monsoons, resisted at first. Then it yielded, and I climbed into the mustiness of a long-closed room, and the wind came in with me, scattering papers across the floor and knocking some unidentifiable object off a table. I closed the window, bolted it again, but the mist crawled through the broken glass, and the wind rattled in it like a pair of castanets.

There were matches in my pocket. I struck three before a light flared up.

I was in a large room, crowded with furniture. Pictures on the walls. Vases on the mantlepiece. A candle stand. And, strangely enough, no cobwebs. For all its external look of neglect and dilapidation, the house had been cared for by someone. But before I could notice anything else, the match burnt out.

As I stepped further into the room, the old deodar flooring creaked beneath my weight. By the light of another match I reached the mantlepiece and lit the candle, noticing at the same time that the candlestick was a genuine antique with cut glass hangings. A deserted cottage with good furniture and glass. I wondered why no one had ever broken in. And then realized that I had just done so.

I held the candlestick high and glanced around the room. The walls were hung with several watercolours and portraits in oils. There was no dust anywhere. But no one answered my call, no one responded to my hesitant knocking. It was as though the occupants of the house were in hiding, watching me obliquely from dark corners and chimneys.

I entered a bedroom and found myself facing a full-length mirror. My reflection stared back at me as though I were a stranger, as though my reflection belonged to the house, while I was only an outsider.

As I turned from the mirror, I thought I saw someone, something, some reflection other than mine, move behind me in the mirror. I caught a glimpse of whiteness, a pale oval face, burning eyes, long tresses, golden in the candlelight. But when

I looked in the mirror again there was nothing to be seen but my own pallid face.

A pool of water was forming at my feet. I set the candle down on a small table, found the edge of the bed—a large old four-poster—sat down, and removed my soggy shoes and socks. Then I took off my clothes and hung them over the back of a chair.

I stood naked in the darkness, shivering a little. There was no one to see me—and yet I felt oddly exposed, almost as though I had stripped in a room full of curious people.

I got under the bedclothes—they smelt slightly of eucalyptus and lavender—but found there was no pillow. That was odd. A perfectly made bed, but no pillow! I was too tired to hunt for one. So I blew out the candle—and the darkness closed in around me, and the whispering began...

The whispering began as soon as I closed my eyes. I couldn't tell where it came from. It was all around me, mingling with the sound of the wind coughing in the chimney, the stretching of old furniture, the weeping of trees outside in the rain.

Sometimes I could hear what was being said. The words came from a distance: a distance not so much of space as of time...

'Mine, mine, he is all mine...'

'He is ours, dear, ours.'

Whispers, echoes, words hovering around me with bats' wings, saying the most inconsequential things with a logical urgency. 'You're late for supper...'

'He lost his way in the mist.'

'Do you think he has any money?'

'To kill a turtle you must first tie its legs to two posts.'

'We could tie him to the bed and pour boiling water down his throat.'

'No, it's simpler this way.'

I sat up. Most of the whispering had been distant, impersonal, but this last remark had sounded horribly near.

I relit the candle and the voices stopped. I got up and prowled around the room, vainly looking for some explanation for the voices. Once again I found myself facing the mirror, staring at my own reflection and the reflection of that other person, the girl with the golden hair and shining eyes. And this time she held a pillow in her hands. She was standing behind me.

I remembered then the stories I had heard as a boy, of two spinster sisters—one beautiful, one plain—who lured rich, elderly gentlemen into their boarding house and suffocated them in the night. The deaths had appeared quite natural, and they had got away with it for years. It was only the surviving sister's deathbed confession that had revealed the truth—and even then no one had believed her.

But that had been many, many years ago, and the house had long since fallen down...

When I turned from the mirror, there was no one behind me. I looked again, and the reflection had gone.

I crawled back into the bed and put the candle out. And I slept and dreamt (or was I awake and did it really happen?) that the woman I had seen in the mirror stood beside the bed, leant over me, looked at me with eyes flecked by orange flames. I saw people moving in those eyes. I saw myself. And then her lips touched mine, lips so cold, so dry, that a shudder ran through my body.

And then, while her face became faceless and only the eyes remained, something else continued to press down upon me, something soft, heavy and shapeless, enclosing me in a suffocating embrace. I could not turn my head or open my mouth. I could not breathe.

I raised my hands and clutched feebly at the thing on top of me. And to my surprise it came away. It was only a pillow that had somehow fallen over my face, half suffocating me while I dreamt of a phantom kiss.

I flung the pillow aside. I flung the bedclothes from me. I had had enough of whispering, of ownerless reflections, of pillows that fell on me in the dark. I would brave the storm outside rather than continue to seek rest in this tortured house.

I dressed quickly. The candle had almost guttered out. The house and everything in it belonged to the darkness of another time; I belonged to the light of day.

I was ready to leave. I avoided the tall mirror with its grotesque rococo design. Holding the candlestick before me, I moved cautiously into the front room. The pictures on the walls sprang to life.

One, in particular, held my attention, and I moved closer to examine it more carefully by the light of the dwindling candle. Was it just my imagination, or was the girl in the portrait the woman of my dream, the beautiful pale reflection in the mirror? Had I gone back in time, or had time caught up with me? Is it time that's passing by, or is it you and I?

I turned to leave, and the candle gave one final sputter and went out, plunging the room in darkness. I stood still for a moment, trying to collect my thoughts, to still the panic that came rushing upon me. Just then, there was a knocking on the door.

'Who's there?' I called.

Silence. And then, again, the knocking, and this time a voice, low and insistent: 'Please let me in, please let me in...'

I stepped forward, unbolted the door, and flung it open.

She stood outside in the rain. Not the pale, beautiful one, but a wizened old hag with bloodless lips and flaring nostrils and—but where were the eyes? No eyes, no eyes!

She swept past me on the wind, and at the same time I took advantage of the open doorway to run outside, to run gratefully into the pouring rain, to be lost for hours among the dripping trees, to be glad for all the leeches clinging to my flesh.

And when, with the dawn, I found my way at last, I rejoiced in birdsong and the sunlight piercing and scattering the clouds.

And today if you were to ask me if the old house is still there or not, I would not be able to tell you, for the simple reason that I haven't the slightest desire to go looking for it.

MY FAR PAVILIONS

Bright red
The poinsettia flames,
As autumn and the old year wanes.

When I have time on my hands, I write haikus, like the one above. This one brings back memories and images of my maternal grandmother's home in Dehra Dun, in the early 1940s. I say grandmother's home because, although grandfather built the house, he had passed on while I was still a child and I have no memories of him that I can conjure up. But he was someone about whom everyone spoke, and I learnt that he had personally supervised the building of the house, partially designing it on the lines of a typical Indian Railways bungalow—neat, compact, and without any frills. None of those Doric pillars, Gothic arches, and mediaeval turrets that characterized some of the Raj house for an earlier period. But instead of the customary red bricks, he used the smooth rounded stones from a local riverbed, and this gave the bungalow a distinctive look.

In all the sixty-five years that I have lived in India, my grandparents' abode was the only house that gave me a feeling of some permanence, as neither my parents nor I were ever to own property. But India was my home, and it was big enough.

Grandfather looked after the mango and lichi orchard at the back of the house, grandmother looked after the flower garden in front. English flowers predominated—philox, larkspur, petunias, sweet peas, snapdragons, nasturtiums; but there was also a jasmine bush, poinsettias, and of course, lots of colourful bougainvillaea climbing the walls. And there were roses brought over from nearby Saharanpur. Saharanpur had become a busy railway junction and an industrial town, but its roses were still famous. It was the home of the botanical survey in northern India, and in the previous century many famous botanists and explorers had ventured into the Himalayas using Saharanpur as their base.

Grandfather had retired from the Railways and settled in Dehra around 1905. At this period, the small foothills town was becoming quite popular as a retreat for retiring Ango-Indian and domiciled Europeans. The bungalows had large compounds and gardens, and Dehra was to remain a garden town until a few years after Independence. The Forest Research Institute, the Survey of India, the Indian Military Academy, and a number of good schools, made the town a special sort of place. By the mid-fifties, the pressures of population meant a greater demand for housing, and gradually the large compounds gave way to housing estates, and the gardens and orchards began to disappear. Most of the estates were now owned by the prospering Indian middle classes. Some of them strove to maintain the town's character and unique charm—flower shows, dog shows, school fetes, club life, dances, garden parties—but gradually these diminished; and today, as the capital of the new state of Uttaranchal, Dehra is as busy, congested and glamorous as any northern town or New Delhi suburb.

My father was always on the move. As a young man, he had been a schoolteacher at Lovedale, in the Nilgiris, then an assistant manager on a tea estate in Travancore-Cochin (now Kerala). He had also worked in the Ichhapore Rifle Factory bordering Calcutta. At the time I was born, he was employed in the Kathiawar states, setting up little schools for the state children in Jamnagar, Pithadia and Jetpur. I grew up in a variety of dwellings, ranging from leaky dak bungalows to spacious palace guest houses. Then, during the Second World War, when he enlisted and was posted in Delhi, we moved from tent to Air Force hutment, to it flat in Scindia House, to rented rooms on Halley Road, Atul Grove, and elsewhere! When he was posted to Karachi, and then Calcutta, I was sent to boarding school in Shimla.

Father had, in fact, grown up in Calcutta, and his mother still lived at 14, Park Lane. She outlived all her children and continued to live at Park Lane until she was almost ninety. Last year, when I visited Calcutta, I found the Park Lane house. But it was boarded up. Nobody seemed to live there any more. Garbage was piled up near the entrance. A billboard hid most of the house from the road.

Possibly my boarding school, Bishop Cotton's in Shimla, provided me with a certain feeling of permanence, especially after I lost my father in 1944. Known as the 'Eton of the East', and run on English public school lines, Bishop Cotton's did not cater to individual privacy. Everyone knew what you kept in your locker. But when I became a senior, I was fortunate enough to be put in charge of the school library. I could use it in my free time, and it became my retreat, where I could read or write or just be on my own. No one bothered me there, for even in those pre-TV and pre-computer days there was no great demand for books! Reading was a minority pastime then, as it is now.

After school, when I was trying to write and sell my early short stories, I found myself ensconced in a tiny barsati, a room on the roof of all old lodging house in Dehra Dun. Alas! Granny's house had been sold by her eldest daugher, who had gone 'home' to England; my stepfather's home was full of half-brothers, stepbrothers and sundry relatives. The barsati gave me privacy.

A bed, a table and a chair were all that the room contained. It was all I needed. Even today, almost fifty years later, my room has the same basic furnishings, except that the table is larger, the bed is slightly more comfortable, and there is a rug on the floor, designed to trip me up whenever I sally forth from the room.

Then, as now, the view from the room, or from its windows, has always been an important factor in my life. I don't think I could stay anywhere for long unless I had a window from which to gaze out upon the world.

Dehra Dun isn't very far from where I live today, and I have passed granny's old bungalow quite often. It is really half a house now, a wall having been built through the centre of the compound. Like the country itself, it found itself partitioned, and there are two owners; one has the lichi trees and the other the mangoes. Good luck to both!

I do not venture in at the gate, I shall keep my memories intact. The only reminders of the past are a couple of potted geraniums on the verandah steps. And I shall sign off with another little haiku:

> *Red geranium*
> *Gleaming against the rain-bright floor...*
> *Memory, hold the door!*

TREES ARE MY BROTHERS

It's good to know that my old friend, the jackfruit, is finally coming into its own. Apparently it is now much in demand in Western countries, a fashionable substitute for meat, being used as fillings for burgers, sandwiches, pies, etc. with one enthusiast even calling it 'mutton hanging from a tree'.

Here in India, we have always appreciated a good jackfruit curry, or even better, a jackfruit pickle. I'm a pickle fiend myself, and among the twenty different pickles on my sideboard there is always a jar of jackfruit pickle; that's why I call it an old friend. But I had no idea it tasted like mutton. The seed and the pulp have their own individual flavour. As it grows on a tree we call it a fruit but we cook it as though it were a vegetable. And if, to some, it tastes like mutton, than perhaps some meat-eaters will become vegetarians. On the other hand, some vegetarians might not care for its meaty flavour!

When I was a boy, we had an old jackfruit tree growing beside the side verandah. I spent a lot of time in the tree surrounding my grandmother's bungalow, and this one was easy to climb. The others included several guava and lichi trees, lemons and grapefruits, and of course a couple of mango trees— but these last were difficult to climb.

'Why do you spend so much time in the trees?' complained

my grandmother. 'Why not do something useful for a change?'

'The trees are my brothers,' I would say, 'I like to play with them.'

And I still think of them as my brothers, although I can no longer climb trees or play in them.

And indeed I think of them as human beings possessed of individuality and charm. Just as no two humans are exactly alike (unless they happen to be twins), so no two trees are the same. Like humans they grow from seed. They develop branches as arms and leaves like flowing hair. We give birth to children, they give birth to fruits and flowers. We shelter our young, they shelter the small creatures of the forest.

But unlike us they spring from the soil, from the land—that very land that gives us food and pasture and protection; the land that we so casually take for granted, preferring to build upon it rather than grow upon it. Where will our cattle graze when the last green spaces, have gone?

'No problem' says a young friend, 'We can always import our milk.'

The other day I came across an old book that had been on my shelves for many years—*Farmer's Glory* by A.G. Street, written over sixty years ago. In his Epilogue he writes: 'It is perhaps nothing to boast about, but there is little doubt that the present prosperity of British farming is mainly due to one man, who is now dead. This name was Adolf Hitler. There is no disputing that it was the fear of famine during the early 1940s which taught the British nation that despite all man's cleverness and inventories, when real danger comes an island people must turn for succour to the only permanent asset they possess, the land of their own country. It has never, and will never, let them down; always provided they realize and obey this eternal truth that to make the land serve man, man must first be content to serve the land.'

And surely it is this love of the land and willingness to serve it that is at the heart of the patriotism. The patriotic songs and speeches that we hear from time to time are fine for stirring up the emotions, but it is really the connect between ourselves and the '*do bigha zameen*' on which we grow our fruit and grain that emboldens us to protect it.

I think I am correct in saying that most of our jawans, the young men who join the solid ranks of the Indian Army, come from rural backgrounds; some from the hills, some from the vast plains and hinterland of our country. They knows the value of the land, they have grown up in villages and have worked with their familiar in the rice fields, or sugar cane plantations, or mango-groves, or wheat or corn or mustard or fields of an infinite variety of crops. More than city folk, they know the value of the land, its true worth in terms of either prosperity or poverty. And so they are ready to defend it, to fight for all its corners. The best soldiers come from the soil that they and their forefathers have tilled.

So let us protect the land—not first from the intruder or the enemy, but from those who would turn the fields or the forest into one more concrete jungle.

But of course there are those who prefer concrete jungles. Like my young friend who wants to live in a Smart City and never mind the cities that are no longer smart. My advice to him (unheeded of course) is to go back to his roots, create a smart little village, and plant jackfruit trees!

GREEN THOUGHTS

Water

I never cease to wonder at the tenacity of water…its ability to make its way through various strata of rock, zigzagging, backtracking, finding space, cunningly discovering faults and fissures in the mountain, and sometimes travelling underground for great distances before emerging into the open. There's no stopping water. For no matter how tiny that little trickle, it has to go somewhere!

◆

If you looked at Earth from a spaceship, you might wonder why we do not call our planet *Water*. Almost three-fourths of the Earth's surface is covered with water, and it is sometimes called the 'water planet'. The oceans, water frozen as ice, lakes and rivers and other surface water, water found underground, water vapour in the atmosphere, and water in all living things make it the most precious of our natural resources.

Your body is about 70 per cent water. All living things, plant and animal, are made of mostly water.

And yet, fresh, pure water is a scarce resource throughout

the world. So treat it with the same respect that you show towards your own body.

◆

Could anything be more delightful than to have a stream or waterfall in your vicinity?

The music of the stream becomes a part of your life. The sounds of daily living might be going on around you, but in the background there is always the soothing sound of water falling over smooth stones. You might be shut away with your work, but always in your mind you will be listening to the stream and your thoughts will wander off to where it passes by green shady banks and meadows sprinkled with daisies and buttercups.

◆

Each drop of water represents a little bit of creation—and of life itself.

When the monsoon brings the first rains of summer, the parched earth opens its pores and quenches its thirst with a hiss of ecstasy. After baking in the sun for several months the land looked cracked, dusty and tired. Now, almost overnight, new grass springs up, there is renewal everywhere, and the wet earth releases a fragrance sweeter than any devised by man.

◆

Trekking in the Himalayan foothills, I came across a patch of green on a rock. Parting a curtain of tender maidenhair fern, I discovered a tiny spring issuing from the rock—nectar for the thirsty traveller!

That same spring, I discovered later, joined other springs to form a swift, tumbling stream, which went cascading down the hill into other rivulets until, in the plains, it became part of a river. And that river flowed into another mightier river...

Be like water, taught La-tze. Soft and limpid, it finds its way through, over or under any obstacle. It does not quarrel; it simply moves on.

◆

Yes, a stream or a small river can be the best, the most intimate of friends. You must love it and live with it before you can really know it.

Living by the sea is quite different. The sea is the beginning and the end, it encompasses all life, for everything must return to it.

In *The Story of My Heart*, my fellow pagan, Richard Jefferies, came close to an understanding with the sea when he wrote: 'Sweet is the bitter sea, and the clear green in which the gaze seeks the soul, looking through the glass into itself. The sea thinks for me as I listen and ponder; the sea thinks, and every boom of the wave repeats my prayer.'

A KNOCK AT THE DOOR

For Sherlock Holmes, it usually meant an impatient client waiting below in the street. For Nero Wolfe, it was the doorbell that rang, disturbing the great man in his orchid rooms. For Poe or Walter de la Mare, that knocking on a moonlit door could signify a ghostly visitor—no one outside!—or, even more mysterious, no one in the house...

Well, clients I have none, and ghostly visitants don't have to knock; but as I spend most of the day at home, writing, I have learnt to live with the occasional knock at the front door. I find doorbells even more startling than ghosts, and ornate brass knockers have a tendency to disappear when the price of brassware goes up; so my callers have to use their knuckles or fists on the solid mahogany door. It's a small price to pay for disturbing me.

I hear the knocking quite distinctly, as the small front room adjoins my even smaller study-cum-bedroom. But sometimes I keep up a pretense of not hearing anything straight away. Mahogany is good for the knuckles! Eventually, I place a pencil between my teeth and holding a sheet of blank foolscap in one hand, move slowly and thoughtfully toward the front door, so that, when I open it, my caller can see that I have been disturbed in the throes of composition. Not that I have ever succeeded in making any one feel guilty about it; they stay as long as they like. And after they have gone, I can get back to listening to my tapes of old Hollywood operettas.

Impervious to both literature and music, my first caller is usually a boy from the village, wanting to sell me his cucumbers or 'France-beans'. For some reason he won't call them French beans. He is not impressed by the accoutrements of my trade. He thrusts a cucumber into my arms and empties the beans on a coffee-table book which has been sent to me for review. (There is no coffee table, but the book makes a good one.) He is confident that I cannot resist his France-beans, even though this sub-Himalayan variety is extremely hard and stringy. Actually, I am a sucker for cucumbers, but I take the beans so I can get the cucumber cheap. In this fashion, authors survive.

The deal done, and the door closed, I decide it's time to do some work. I start this little essay. If it's nice and gets published, I will be able to take care of the electricity bill. There's a knock at the door. Some knocks I recognize, but this is a new one. Perhaps it's someone asking for a donation. Cucumber in hand, I stride to the door and open it abruptly only to be confronted by a polite, smart-looking chauffeur who presents me with a large bouquet of flowering gladioli!

'With the compliments of Mr B.P. Singh,' he announces, before departing smartly with a click of the heels. I start looking for a receptacle for the flowers, as Grandmother's flower vase was really designed for violets and forget-me-nots.

B.P. Singh is a kind man who had the original idea of turning his property outside Mussoorie into a gladioli farm. A bare hillside is now a mass of gladioli from May to September. He sells them to flower shops in Delhi, but his heart bleeds at harvesting time.

Gladioli arranged in an ice bucket, I return to my desk and

am just wondering what I should be writing next, when there is a loud banging on the door. No friendly knock this time. Urgent, peremptory, summoning! Could it be the police? And what have I gone and done? Every good citizen has at least one guilty secret, just waiting to be discovered! I move warily to the door and open it an inch or two. It is a policeman!

Hastily, I drop the cucumber and politely ask him if I can be of help. Try to look casual, I tell myself. He has a small packet in his hands. No, it's not a warrant. It turns out to be a slim volume of verse, sent over by a visiting DIG of Police, who has authored it. I thank his emissary profusely, and, after he has gone, I place the volume reverently on my bookshelf, beside the works of other poetry-loving policemen. These men of steel, who inspire so much awe and trepidation in the rest of us, they too are humans and some of them are poets!

Now it's afternoon, and the knock I hear is a familiar one, and welcome, for it heralds the postman. What would writers do without postmen? They have more power than literary agents. I don't have an agent (I'll be honest and say an agent won't have me), but I do have a postman, and he turns up every day except when there's a landslide.

Yes, it's Prakash the postman who makes my day, showering me with letters, books, acceptances, rejections, and even the occasional cheque. These postmen are fine fellows, they do their utmost to bring the good news from Ghent to Aix.

And what has Prakash brought me today? A reminder: I haven't paid my subscription to the Author's Guild. I'd better send it off, or I shall be a derecognized author. A letter from a reader: would I like to go through her 800-page dissertation on the Gita? Some day, my love... A cheque, a cheque! From Sunflower Books, for nineteen rupees only, representing the sale of six copies of one of my books during the previous year.

Never mind. Six wise persons put their money down for my book. No fresh acceptances, but no rejections either. A postcard from Goa, where one of my publishers is taking a holiday. So the post is something of an anticlimax. But I mustn't complain. Not every knock on the door brings gladioli fresh from the fields. Tomorrow's another day, and the postman comes six days a week.

THE YEAR OF THE KISSING AND OTHER GOOD TIMES

' Seeds of the potato-berries should be sown in adapted places by explorers of new countries.'

So declared a botanically-minded empire-builder. And among those who took this advice was Captain Young of the Sirmur Rifles, Commandant of the Doon from the end of the Gurkha War in 1815 to the time of the Mutiny (1857).

It has to be said that the good captain was motivated by self-interest. He was an Irishman and fond of potatoes. He liked his Irish stew. So he grew his own potatoes and encouraged the good people of Garhwal to grow them too. In 1823, he received a supply of superior Irish potatoes and was considering where to plant them. The northern hill districts had been in British hands for almost ten years, but as yet no one had thought of resorting to them for rest or relaxation. The hills of central India, covered with jungle, were known to be extremely unhealthy. The Siwaliks near Dehra Dun were malarious. It was supposed that the Himalayan foothills, also forest clad, would be equally unhealthy. But Captain Young was to discover otherwise.

Carrying his beloved Irish potatoes with him, Captain

Young set out on foot and soon left the subtropical Doon behind him. Above 4,000 feet he came to forests of oak and rhododendron, and above 6,000 feet they found cedars, known in the Himalayas as deodars or devdars—trees of the gods. He found a climate so cool and delightful that not only did he plant potatoes, he built himself a small hunting lodge facing the snows.

Captain Young was to make a number of visits to his little hut on the mountain. No one lived nearby. The villages were situated in the valleys, where water was available. Bears, leopards and wild boar roamed the forests. There were pheasants in the shady ravines and small trout in the little Aglar river. Young and his companions could hunt and fish to their hearts content. In 1826 Young, now a Colonel, built the first large house, 'Mullingar' (I see its remnants from my window every morning), on the way up to what became the convalescent depot and cantonment. Others soon began to follow Young's example, settling as far away as Cloud End and The Abbey. By 1830, the twin hill stations of Landour and Mussoorie had come into being.

Those early pleasure-seeking residents took little or no interest in potato growing, but Young certainly did, and the slope beneath his house became known as Colonel Young's potato field. You won't find potatoes there now, only Professor Saili's dahlias and cucumbers; but potato growing had caught on with the farmers in the surrounding villages, and soon everyone in Garhwal and beyond was growing potatoes.

The potato, practically unknown in India before its introduction in the nineteenth century, was soon to become a popular and vital ingredient of so many Indian dishes. The humble aloo made life much more interesting for chefs, housewives, gourmands and gourmets. The writers of cookery books would have a hard time filling out their pages without the help of the potato.

> For aloo-mutter and aloo-dhum,
> Our heartfelt thanks to Captain Young!

Shimla became the capital of British India, Nainital the capital of the United Provinces. These towns were soon teeming with officials and empire-builders. But Mussoorie remained non-official, the pleasure capital of the princes, wealthy Indians, European entrepreneurs, and the wives and mistresses of all of them. Mussoorie was smaller than Shimla, all length and not much width, but there was room enough for private lives, for discreet affairs conducted over picnic baskets beneath the whispering deodars.

Ah, those picnics! They seem to be a thing of the past, now that you can drive almost anywhere and find a line of dhabas awaiting you. Few people today bother to prepare those delicate sandwiches or delicious parathas when packets of potato chips and other fast foods are to be found at every bend of the road. Stop at any dhaba in the hills and an instant meal of chow mein will be ready for you. Professor Saili tells me that chow mein is now the national dish of Uttaranchal. I believe him. My own family members demand it whenever we are out for the day.

But to return to Mussoorie's easy-going early days, before the missionaries arrived and made their own rules, imposing their ideas of morality upon the inhabitants.

The station's reputation was well-established as far back as October 1884, when the local correspondent of the Calcutta *Statesman* wrote to his paper: 'Last Sunday, a sermon was delivered by the Rev Mr Hackett, belonging to the Church Mission society; he chose for his text Ezekiel

18th and 2nd verse, the latter clause: "The fathers have eaten sour grapes and set their children's teeth on edge." The reverend gentleman discoursed upon the highly immoral tone of society up here, that it far surpassed any other hill station in the scale of morals; that ladies and gentlemen after attending church proceeded to a drinking shop, a restaurant adjoining the library and there indulged freely in pegs, not one but many; that at a Fancy Bazaar held this season, a lady stood up on a chair and offered her kisses to gentlemen at ₹5 each. What would they think of such a state of society at Home? But this was not all. Married ladies and married gents formed friendships and associations, which tended to no good purpose, and set a bad example.'

Adultery under the pines? Mussoorie was well ahead of the times. The poor reverend preached to no purpose. And it was just as well that he was not alive in the year 1933, when a lady stood up at a benefit show and auctioned a single kiss, for which a gentleman paid ₹300, a substantial amount seventy years ago. (A year's house rent, in fact.) The *Statesman*'s correspondent had nothing to say on this latter occasion; his silence was in itself a comment on the changing times.

A few years ago I received a letter from a reader in England, wanting to know if there were any Maxwells still living in Mussoorie. He was a Maxwell himself, he said, by his father's first marriage. From what he knew of the family history, there ought to have been several Maxwells by the second marriage, and he wanted to get in touch with them.

He was very frank and mentioned that his father had given up a brilliant career in the Indian Civil Service to marry a fourteen-year-old Muslim girl. He had met her in Madras, changed his religion to facilitate the marriage, and then—to avoid 'scandal'—had made his home with her in Mussoorie.

Although there are no longer any Maxwells living in Mussoorie, my former neighbour, Miss Bean, confirmed that Mr Maxwell's children from his second wife had grown up on the hillside, each inheriting a considerable property. The children emigrated, but one granddaughter returned to Mussoorie not so long ago, on a honeymoon with her fourth husband, thus keeping up the family tradition.

Mussoorie was probably at its brightest and gayest in the 1930s. Ballrooms, skating rinks and cinema halls flourished. Beauty saloons sprang up along the Mall. An old advertisement in my possession announces the superiority of Madame Freda in the art of 'permanent waving'. Another old ad recommends Holloway's Ointment as a 'certain remedy for bad legs, bad breasts, and ulcerations of all kinds.'

Darlington's Pain-Curer was another certain remedy for all manner of ailments. It was even recommended by His Highness Raja Pratap Sah of Tehri-Garhwal State, whose domains bordered Mussoorie: 'It affords me much pleasure in informing you that the two bottles of Darlington's Pain-Curer, which I took from you, has given extraordinary relief from the rheumatism I have been suffering since last six months. Therefore I request you to send me two bottles more (large size) as I wish to take this valuable medicine with me on my tour through the Himalaya mountains.'

Neither the ad nor his Highness tells us whether you were supposed to apply the potion or drink the stuff. Perhaps you could do both.

By the time Independence came to India, most of the British and Anglo-Indian residents of our hill stations had sold their homes and left the country. Only a few stayed on—elderly folks like Miss Bean who had spent all their lives here and whose meagre incomes did not allow them to settle abroad.

I wonder what really brought me to Mussoorie in the 1960s. True, I had been here as a child, and my mother's people had lived in Dehra Dun, in the valley below. When I returned to India, still a young man in my twenties (I had spent only four years in England), I lived in Delhi and Dehra Dun for a few years; and then, on an impulse, I found myself revisiting the hill station, calling on the oldest resident, Miss Bean, and being told by her that the upper portion of her cottage, Maplewood, was to let. On another impulse, I rented it.

Always a creature of impulse, my life has been shaped more by a benign providence than by any system of foresight or planning.

Well, that was forty years ago, and Miss Bean has long since gone to her Maker, and here I am in the midst of a large family, living in another cottage and doing my best to keep it from falling down.

Perhaps I really wanted to come back to my beginnings. Because it was in Mussoorie in 1933 (the Year of the Kissing!) that my parents met each other and were married.

I have a photograph of them, on horseback, riding on the Camel's Back Road. He was thirty-six then and had just given up a tea-estate manager's job; she was barely twenty, taking a nurse's training at the Cottage Hospital, just below Gun Hill. A few months later they were living in the heat and dust of Alwar, in Rajasthan, and then Jamnagar in Kathiawar, where my father conducted a small palace school. I was not born in Mussoorie but I am pretty sure I had my conception there!

There is something in the air of the place—especially in October—that is conducive to love and passion and desire. Miss Bean told me that as a girl she'd many suitors, and if she did not marry it was more from procrastination than from being passed over. While on all sides elopements and broken marriages were making hill station life exciting, and providing orphans and illegitimate children for the mission schools, Miss Bean contrived to remain single and childless. She was probably helped by the fact of her father being a retired police officer with a reputation for being a good shot with the pistol and Lee-Enfield rifle.

She taught elocution in one of the many schools that flourished (and still flourish) in Mussoorie. There is a protective atmosphere about a residential school, an atmosphere which, although it protects one from the outside would, often exposes one to the hazards within the system.

The schools were not without their own scandals. Mrs Fennimore, the wife of a headmaster at Oak Grove, got herself entangled in a defamation suit, each hearing of which grew more and more distasteful to her husband. Unable to stand the whole weary and sordid business, Mr Fennimore hit upon a solution. Loading his revolver, he moved to his wife's bedside and shot her through the head. For no accountable reason he put the weapon under her pillow—obviously no one could have mistaken the death for suicide—and then, going to his study, he leaned over his rifle and shot himself.

Ten years later, in the same school, another headmaster's wife was arrested for attempted murder. She had fired at, and wounded a junior mistress. The motive remained obscure and the case was hushed up.

In the St. Fidelis' School, circa 1941, a boy asleep in the dormitory had his throat slit by another boy, it was said at the instigation of one of the teachers. This too was hushed up, but the school closed down a year later.

In recent years, there has been a suicide in one public school, and murders (involving students) in two others; also an accidental death by way of a drug overdose. Tom Brown's school days were pretty dull when compared to the goings-on in some of our residential schools.

These affairs usually get hushed up, but there was no hushing up the incidents that took place on the 25 July 1927, at the height of the season and in the heart of the town—a double tragedy that set the station agog with excitement. It all happened in broad daylight and in a full boarding house, Zephyr Hall.

Shortly after noon the boarders were startled into brisk activity when a shot rang out from one of the rooms, followed by screams. Other shots followed in quick succession. Those boarders who happened to be in the lounge or on the verandah dived for the safety of their own rooms and bolted the doors. One unhappy boarder however, ignorant of where the man with the gun might be, decided to take no chances and came around the corner with his hands held well above his head only to run straight into the levelled pistol! Even the man who held it, and who had just shot his wife and daughter, couldn't help laughing.

Mr Owen, the maniac with the gun, after killing his wife and wounding his daughter finally shot himself. His was the first official Christian cremation in Mussoorie, performed apparently in compliance with wishes expressed long before his dramatic end.

A couple of years ago I had a letter from an old Mussoorie resident, Col. Cole, now retired in Pune, who recalled the event: 'Mrs Owen ran Zephyr Hall as a boarding house. It was the last Saturday of the month, and Mrs Owen's son Basil was with me at the 11 a.m.–1 p.m. session at the skating rink and so escaped the tragedy that took place about midday, when Mr Owen shot Mrs Owen and one daughter and then shot himself. I do not know what happened to Basil but he was withdrawn from school and an uncle took him over. This was not the end of the family tragedy. An older sister of Basil's in her early twenties was boating on the river Gumpti at Lucknow with her fiance, when a flash flood took place and the strong current drowned them both.'

This was not the end of the story, at least not for me.

A few summers ago, while I was walking along the Mall, I was stopped by a stranger, a small man with pale blue eyes and thinning hair. He must have been over sixty. Accompanying him was a much younger woman, whom he introduced as his wife. He apologized for detaining me, and said: 'You look as though you have been here a long time. Do you know if any of the Gantzers still live here? I believe they look after the cemetery.'

I gave him the necessary directions and then asked him if he was visiting Mussoorie for the first time. He seemed to welcome the inquiry and showed a willingness to talk.

'It's well over fifty years since I was last here', he said. 'I was just a boy at the time'. And he gestured towards the ruins of Zephyr Hall, now occupied by postmen and their families. 'That was my mother's boarding house. That was where she died...'

'Not-not Mr Owen?' I ventured to ask.

'That's right. So you've heard about it. My father had a sudden brainstorm. He shot and killed Mother. My sister was badly wounded. I was out at the time. Now I have come to revisit her grave. I know she'd have wanted me to come.'

He took my telephone number and promised to look me up before he left Mussoorie. But I did not see him again. After a few days, I began to wonder if I had really met a survivor of this old tragedy, or if he had been just another of the hill station's ghosts. But one day, while I was walking along the cemetery's lowest terrace, I found confirmation that Mrs Owen's son had indeed visited his mother's grave. Set into the tombstone was a new stone plaque with the inscription: '*Mother Dear, I am Here.*'

AND NOW WE ARE TWELVE

People often ask me why I've chosen to live in Mussoori for so long—almost forty years without any significant breaks.

'I forgot to go away,' I tell them, but of course, that isn't the real reason.

The people here are friendly, but then people are friendly in a great many other places. The hills, the valleys are beautiful; but they are just as beautiful in Kulu or Kumaon.

'This is where the family has grown up and where we all live,' I say, and those who don't know me are puzzled because the general impression of the writer is of a reclusive old bachelor.

Unmarried I may be, but single I am not. Not since Prem came to live and work with me in 1970. A year later, he was married. Then his children came along and stole my heart; and when they grew up, their children came along and stole my wits. So now I'm an enchanted bachelor, head of a family of twelve. Sometimes I go out to bat, sometimes to bowl, but generally I prefer to be twelfth man, carrying out the drinks!

In the old days, when I was a solitary writer living on baked beans, the prospect of my suffering from obesity was very remote. Now there is a little more of author than there used to be, and the other day five-year-old Gautam patted me on my tummy (or balcony, as I prefer to call it) and remarked:

'Dada, you should join the WWE.'

'I'm already a member,' I said, 'I joined the World Wildlife Fund years ago.'

'Not that,' he said. 'I mean the World Wrestling Federation.'

If I have a tummy today, it's thanks to Gautam's grandfather and now his mother who, over the years, have made sure that I am well-fed and well-proportioned.

Forty years ago, when I was a lean young man, people would look at me and say, 'Poor chap, he's definitely undernourished. What on earth made him take up writing as a profession?' Now they look at me and say, 'You wouldn't think he was a writer, would you? Too well-nourished!'

◆

It was a cold, wet and windy March evening when Prem came back from the village with his wife and first-born child, then just four months old. In those days, they had to walk to the house from the bus stand; it was a half-hour walk in the cold rain, and the baby was all wrapped up when they entered the front room. Finally, I got a glimpse of him, and he of me, and it was friendship at first sight. Little Rakesh (as he was to be called) grabbed me by the nose and held on. He did not have much of a nose to grab, but he had a dimpled chin and I played with it until he smiled.

The little chap spent a good deal of his time with me during those first two years of his in Maplewood—learning to crawl, to toddle, and then to walk unsteadily about the little sitting room. I would carry him into the garden, and later, up the steep gravel path to the main road. Rakesh enjoyed these little excursions, and so did I, because in pointing out trees, flowers, birds, butterflies, beetles, grasshoppers, et al, I was giving myself a chance to observe them better instead of just taking them for granted.

In particular, there was a pair of squirrels that lived in the big oak tree outside the cottage. Squirrels are rare in Mussoorie though common enough down in the valley. This couple must have come up for the summer. They became quite friendly, and although they never got around to taking food from our hands, they were soon entering the house quite freely. The sitting room window opened directly on to the oak tree whose various denizens—ranging from stag-beetles to small birds and even an acrobatic bat—took to darting in and out of the cottage at various times of the day or night.

Life at Maplewood was quite idyllic, and when Rakesh's baby brother, Suresh, came into the world, it seemed we were all set for a long period of domestic bliss; but at such times, tragedy is often lurking just around the corner. Suresh was just over a year old when he contracted tetanus. Doctors and hospitals were of no avail. He suffered—as any child would from this terrible affliction—and left this world before he had a chance of getting to know it. His parents were broken-hearted. And I feared for Rakesh, for he wasn't a very healthy boy, and two of his cousins in the village had already succumbed to tuberculosis.

It was to be a difficult year for me. A criminal charge was brought against me for a slightly risque story I'd written for a Bombay magazine. I had to face trial in Bombay and this involved three journeys there over a period of a year and a half, before an irate but perceptive judge found the charges baseless and gave me an honourable acquittal.

It's the only time I've been involved with the law and I sincerely hope it is the last. Most cases drag on interminably, and the main beneficiaries are the lawyers. My trial would have been much longer had not the prosecutor died of a heart attack in the middle of the proceedings. His successor did not pursue it with the same vigour. His heart was not in it. The whole issue had started with a complaint by a local politician, and when he lost interest, so did the prosecution. Nevertheless, the trial, once begun, had to be seen through. The defence (organized by the concerned magazine) marshalled its witnesses (which included Nissim Ezekiel and the Marathi playwright Vijay Tendulkar). I made a short speech which couldn't have been very memorable as I have forgotten it! And everyone, including the judge, was bored with the whole business. After that, I steered clear of controversial publications. I have never set out to shock the world. Telling a meaningful story was all that really mattered. And that is still the case.

I was looking forward to continuing our idyllic existence in Maplewood, but it was not to be. The powers-that-be, in the shape of the Public Works Department (PWD), had decided to build a 'strategic' road just below the cottage and without any warning to us, all the trees in the vicinity were felled (including the friendly old oak) and the hillside was rocked by explosives and bludgeoned by bulldozers. I decided it was time to move. Prem and Chandra (Rakesh's mother) wanted to move too; not because of the road, but because they associated the house with the death of little Suresh, whose presence seemed to haunt every room, every corner of the cottage. His little cries of pain and suffering still echoed through the still hours of the night.

I rented rooms at the top of Landour, a good thousand feet higher up the mountain. Rakesh was now old enough to go to school, and every morning I would walk with him down to the little convent school near the clock tower. Prem would go to fetch him in the afternoon. The walk took us about half an hour, and on the way Rakesh would ask for a story and I would have to rack my brains in order to invent one. I am not the most inventive of writers, and fantastical plots are beyond me. My forte is observation, recollection, and reflection. Small boys prefer action. So I invented a leopard who suffered from acute indigestion because he'd eaten one human too many and a belt buckle was causing an obstruction.

This went down quite well until Rakesh asked me how the leopard got around the problem of the victim's clothes.

'The secret,' I said, 'is to pounce on them when their trousers are off!'

Not the stuff of which great picture books are made, but then, I've never attempted to write stories for beginners. Red Riding Hood's granny-eating wolf always scared me as a small boy, and yet parents have always found it acceptable for toddlers. Possibly they feel grannies are expendable.

Mukesh was born around this time and Savitri (Dolly) a couple of years later. When Dolly grew older, she was annoyed at having been named Savitri (my choice), which is now considered very old-fashioned; so we settled for Dolly. I can understand a child's dissatisfaction with given names. My first name was Owen, which in Welsh means 'brave'. As I am not in the least brave, I have preferred not to use it. One given name and one surname should be enough.

When my granny said, 'But you should try to be brave, otherwise how will you survive in this cruel world?' I replied:

'Don't worry, I can run very fast.'

Not that I've ever had to do much running, except when I was pursued by a lissome Australian lady who thought I'd make a good obedient husband. It wasn't so much the lady I was running from, but the prospect of spending the rest of my life in some remote cattle station in the Australian outback. Anyone who has tried to drag me away from India has always met with stout resistance.

♦

Up on the heights of Landour lived a motley crowd. My immediate neighbours included a Frenchwoman who played the sitar (very badly) all through the night; a Spanish lady with two husbands. One of whom practised acupuncture—rather ineffectively as far as he was concerned, for he seemed to be dying of some mysterious debilitating disease. The other came and went rather mysteriously, and finally ended up in Tihar Jail, having been apprehended at Delhi airport carrying a large amount of contraband hashish.

Apart from these and a few other colourful characters, the area was inhabited by some very respectable people, retired brigadiers, air marshals and rear admirals, almost all of whom were busy writing their memoirs. I had to read or listen to extracts from their literary efforts. This was slow torture. A few years before, I had done a stint of editing for a magazine called *Imprint*. It had involved going through hundreds of badly written manuscripts, and in some cases (friends of the owner!) rewriting some of them for publication. One of life's joys had been to throw up that particular job, and now here I was, besieged by all the top brass of the Army, Navy and Air Force, each one determined that I should read, inwardly digest, improve, and if possible find a publisher for their outpourings. Thank goodness they were all retired. I could not be shot or court-martialled. But at least two of them set their wives upon me, and these intrepid ladies would turn up around noon with my 'homework'—typescripts to read and edit! There was no escape. My own writing was of no consequence to them. I told them that I was taking sitar lessons, but they disapproved, saying I was more suited to the tabla.

When Prem discovered a set of vacant rooms further down the Landour slope, close to school and bazaar, I rented them without hesitation. This was Ivy Cottage. Come up and see me sometimes, but leave your manuscripts behind.

When we came to Ivy Cottage in 1980, we were six, Dolly having just been born. Now, twenty-four years later, we are twelve. I think that's a reasonable expansion. The increase has been brought about by Rakesh's marriage twelve years ago, and Mukesh's marriage two years ago. Both precipitated themselves into marriage when they were barely twenty, and both were lucky. Beena and Binita, who happen to be real sisters, have brightened and enlivened our lives with their happy, positive natures and the wonderful children they have brought into the world. More about them later.

Ivy Cottage has, on the whole, been kind to us, and particularly kind to me. Some houses like their occupants, others don't. Maplewood, set in the shadow of the hill lacked a natural cheerfulness; there was a settled gloom about the place. The house at the top of Landour was too exposed to the elements to have any sort of character. The wind moaning in the deodars may have inspired the sitar player but it did nothing for my writing. I produced very little up there. On the other hand, Ivy Cottage—especially my little room facing the sunrise— has been conducive to creative work. Novellas, poems, essays, children's stories, anthologies, have all come tumbling on to whatever sheets of paper happen to be nearest me. As I write by hand, I have only to grab for the nearest pad, loose sheet, page-proof or envelope whenever the muse takes hold of me; which is surprisingly often.

I came here when I was nearing fifty. Now I'm seventy, and instead of drying up, as some writers do in their later years, I find myself writing with as much ease and assurance as when I was twenty. And I enjoy writing. It's not a burdensome task. I may not have anything of earth-shattering significance to convey to the world, but in conveying my sentiments to you, dear readers, and in telling you something about my relationship with people and the natural world, I hope to bring a little pleasure and sunshine into your life.

Life isn't a bed of roses, not for any of us, and I have never had the comforts or luxuries that wealth can provide. But here I am, doing my own thing, in my own time and my own way. What more can I ask of life? Give me a big cash prize and I'd still be here. I happen to like the view from my window. And I like to have Gautam coming up to me, patting me on the tummy, and telling me that I'll make a good goalkeeper one day.

It's a Sunday morning, as I come to the conclusion of this chapter. There's bedlam in the house. Siddharth's football keeps smashing against the front door. Shrishti is practising her dance routine in the back verandah. Gautam has cut his finger and is trying his best to bandage it with sellotape. He is, of course, the youngest of Rakesh's three musketeers, and probably the most independent-minded. Siddharth, now ten, is restless, never quite able to expend all his energy. 'Does not pay enough attention,' says his teacher. It must be hard for anyone to pay attention in a class of sixty! How does the poor teacher pay attention?

If you, dear reader, have any ambitions to be a writer, you must first rid yourself of any notion that perfect peace and quiet is the first requirement. There is no such thing as perfect peace and quiet except perhaps in a monastery or a cave in the mountains. And what would you write about, living in a cave? One should be able to write in a train, a bus, a bullock-cart, in good weather or bad, on a park bench or in the middle of a noisy classroom.

Of course, the best place is the sun-drenched desk right next to my bed. It isn't always sunny here, but on a good day like this, it's ideal. The children are getting ready for school, dogs are barking in the street, and down near the water tap there's an altercation between two women with empty buckets, the tap having dried up. But these are all background noises and will subside in due course. They are not directed at me.

Hello! Here's Atish, Mukesh's little ten-month old infant, crawling over the rug, curious to know why I'm sitting on the edge of my bed scribbling away, when I should be playing with him. So I shall play with him for five minutes and then come back to this page. Giving him my time is important. After all, I won't be around when he grows up.

Half-an-hour later. Atish soon tired of playing with me, but meanwhile Gautam had absconded with my pen. When I asked him to return it, he asked, 'Why don't you get a computer? Then we can play games on it.'

'My pen is faster than any computer,' I tell him, 'I wrote three pages this morning without getting out of bed. And yesterday I wrote two pages sitting under Billoo's chestnut tree.'

'Until a chestnut fell on your head,' says Gautam, 'Did it hurt?'

'Only a little,' I said, putting on a brave front.

He had saved the chestnut and now he showed it to me. The smooth brown horse-chestnut shone in the sunlight.

'Let's stick it in the ground,' I said. 'Then in the spring a chestnut tree will come up.'

So we went outside and planted the chestnut on a plot of wasteland. Hopefully a small tree will burst through the earth at about the time this little book is published.

THE NIGHT THE ROOF BLEW OFF

We are used to sudden storms up here on the first range of the Himalayas. The old building in which we live has, for more than a hundred years, received the full force of the wind as it sweeps across the hills from the east.

We'd lived in the building for more than ten years without a disaster. It had even taken the shock of a severe earthquake. As my granddaughter Dolly said, 'It's difficult to tell the new cracks from the old!'

It's a two-storey building, and I live on the upper floor with my family: my three grandchildren and their parents. The roof is made of corrugated tin sheets, the ceiling of wooden boards. That's the traditional Mussoorie roof.

Looking back at the experience, it was the sort of thing that should have happened in a James Thurber story, like the dam that burst or the ghost who got in. But I wasn't thinking of Thurber at the time, although a few of his books were among the many I was trying to save from the icy rain pouring into my bedroom.

Our roof had held fast in many a storm, but the wind that night was really fierce. It came rushing at us with a high-pitched, eerie wail. The old roof groaned and protested. It took a battering for several hours while the rain lashed against the windows and the lights kept coming and going.

There was no question of sleeping, but we remained in bed for warmth and comfort. The fire had long since gone out as the chimney had collapsed, bringing down a shower of sooty rainwater.

After about four hours of buffeting, the roof could take it no longer. My bedroom faces east, so my portion of the roof was the first to go.

The wind got under it and kept pushing until, with a ripping, groaning sound, the metal sheets shifted and slid off the rafters, some of them dropping with claps like thunder on to the road below.

So that's it, I thought. Nothing worse can happen. As long as the ceiling stays on, I'm not getting out of bed. We'll collect our roof in the morning.

Icy water splashing down on my face made me change my mind in a hurry. Leaping from the bed, I found that much of the ceiling had gone, too. Water was pouring on my open typewriter as well as on the bedside radio and bedcover.

Picking up my precious typewriter (my companion for forty years) I stumbled into the front sitting room (and library), only to find a similar situation there. Water was pouring through the slats of the wooden ceiling, raining down on the open bookshelves.

By now I had been joined by the children, who had come to my rescue. Their section of the roof hadn't gone as yet. Their parents were struggling to close a window against the driving rain.

'Save the books!' shouted Dolly, the youngest, and that became our rallying cry for the next hour or two.

Dolly and her brother Mukesh picked up armfuls of books and carried them into their room. But the floor was awash, so the books had to be piled on their beds. Dolly was helping me gather some of my papers when a large field rat jumped on to the desk in front of her. Dolly squealed and ran for the door.

'It's all right,' said Mukesh, whose love of animals extends even to field rats. 'It's only sheltering from the storm.'

Big brother Rakesh whistled for our dog, Tony, but Tony wasn't interested in rats just then. He had taken shelter in the kitchen, the only dry spot in the house.

Two rooms were now practically roofless, and we could see the sky lit up by flashes of lightning.

There were fireworks indoors, too, as water spluttered and crackled along a damaged wire. Then the lights went out altogether.

Rakesh, at his best in an emergency, had already lit two kerosene lamps. And by their light we continued to transfer books, papers, and clothes to the children's room.

We noticed that the water on the floor was beginning to subside a little.

'Where is it going?' asked Dolly.

'Through the floor,' said Mukesh. 'Down to the flat below!'

Cries of concern from our downstairs neighbours told us that they were having their share of the flood.

Our feet were freezing because there hadn't been time to put on proper footwear. And besides, shoes and slippers were awash by now. All chairs and tables were piled high with books. I hadn't realized the extent of my library until that night!

The available beds were pushed into the driest corner of the children's room, and there, huddled in blankets and quilts, we spent the remaining hours of the night while the storm continued.

Towards morning the wind fell, and it began to snow. Through the door to the sitting room I could see snowflakes drifting through the gaps in the ceiling, settling on picture frames. Ordinary things like a glue bottle and a small clock took on a certain beauty when covered with soft snow.

Most of us dozed off.

When dawn came, we found the windowpanes encrusted with snow and icicles. The rising sun struck through the gaps in the ceiling and turned everything golden. Snow crystals glistened on the empty bookshelves. But the books had been saved.

Rakesh went out to find a carpenter and tinsmith, while the rest of us started putting things in the sun to dry. By evening, we'd put much of the roof back on.

It's a much-improved roof now, and we look forward to the next storm with confidence!

THOUGHTS ON PASSING EIGHTY

There is nothing special about living into one's eighties. Many people do it. I can't say that I am any better, or any wiser, for having passed this landmark. But I must say I am a little surprised, because I do not came from a long-lived family (both parents and two grandparents having died quiet young); nor have I bothered to take care of myself, health-wise. And I hate all forms of physical exercise!

No jogging for me. No climbing mountain peaks. No dumbbells or bullworkers or those machines that make you run in one place. I hate running. I will run only when chased by a madman or a mad bull. At school, I came last in the marathon, having stopped along the way to partake of refreshments made available by enterprising vendors of roasted peanuts or bhuttas.

Yoga? No, I am not a yoga enthusiast. I do admire people who can tie themselves into knots, but I am a peculiarly un-knotty person, liable to be stuck in one position for hours if I try too ambitious an asana. (Is that the right word?) Some years ago I tried looping my right leg over my left shoulder, only to end up calling for help. As ten-year-old Gautam disentangled me, he said: 'You looked like a semicolon, Dada. You should stick to writing.'

Stick to writing! Good advice from a preteen. And I am

frequently taking advice from children. Such as: 'Don't cut your hair too short, Dada, girls like it long.' These little tips go a long way in helping me to win friends and influence people.

But why am I writing this essay? Because only the other day, at our local bookshop, a young man came up to me and said: 'Sir, tell me—what is the secret to happiness?' It was hardly the time for homespun philosophy, as a pretty young thing was trying to take a selfie of the two of us, so all I could say was:

'Signing books for young readers. It would make any writer happy.'

'But I'm not a writer,' he said, 'I'm a psychiatrist.'

'Well then, make your patients happy,' was all I could say.

Which reminds me—when I was a young man and thought I know the answers to everything, I wrote a piece called 'Thoughts on Reaching Thirty'. It was published in *The Illustrated Weekly of India*, a great magazine now long extinct.

And what were my thoughts at thirty? They couldn't have been very profound, because I can't remember even one of them! And yet, at that enquiring age, I was under the influence of Spritualism, Theosophy, Taoism, Christian Science, and the teachings of Gurdjieff!

I suppose the sum of all these things had some effect on me, because the landmark ages of forty, fifty, sixty and seventy passed without any age to put down my great thoughts—if, indeed, there were any.

Meditation? This was once recommended to me by a gentleman in Rishikesh who had been meditating beside the Ganga for several years. (He had a settled income, which meant he did not have to work for a living.) Well, I do try a little meditation from time to time. The trouble is, after a few minutes I fall asleep.

You see, I have this wonderful ability to fall asleep at any given moment, and it is probably the secret of my happiness. I can sleep by night, I can sleep by day. I can sleep in the sun, I can sleep in the shade. I can sleep in my bed, I can sleep on the back of an elephant. (I have yet to try a camel).

Perhaps I am meditating in the wrong place. My little room, with the morning sun on my desk, is really meant for writing—or sleeping. In between naps I write stories or little essays like this one. If I am to meditate successfully, I should be down in Rishikesh like my friend on the banks of the Ganga.

When I was a boy I would occasionally visit Haridwar, sometimes in the company of my lost friend Kishen. In my first novel, *The Room on the Roof,* I have described how we crossed the Ganga in a small boat accompanied by a number of pilgrims all chanting: '*Ganga-mai ki jai!*' It was a moving experience both in my story and in reality. And whenever I visited Haridwar, I would sing out '*Ganga-mai ki jai!*' with whoever was with me.

I am not a religious person, but I have always been moved by the devotion of others. Every evening, after Beena (my granddaughter) has done her puja, she brings me prasad, and I accept it humbly and gratefully because it is the symbol of her goodness and devotion. To light a candle is better than to curse the darkness.

And so here I am, in my eighties, trying to gather my thoughts and to see if I have any *great* thoughts. But none come to me. You must do your own thinking, dear reader.

MOTHER HILL

It is hard to realize that I've been here all these years—twenty-five summers, winters and Himalayan springs. When I look back to the time of my first coming here, it does seem like yesterday.

That probably sums it all up. Time passes, and yet it doesn't pass; people come and go, the mountains remain. Mountains are permanent things. They are stubborn, they refuse to move. You can blast holes out of them for their mineral wealth, strip them of their trees and foliage, or dam their streams and divert their currents. You can make tunnels and roads and bridges; but no matter how hard they try, humans cannot actually get rid of the mountains. That's what I like about them; they are here to stay.

I like to think that I have become a part of these mountains, this particular range, and that by living here for so long, I am able to claim a relationship with the trees, wild flowers, and even the rocks that are an integral part of it.

Yesterday at twilight, when I passed beneath a canopy of oak leaves, I felt that I was a part of the forest. I put out my hand and touched the bark of an old tree, and as I turned away, its leaves brushed against my face as if to acknowledge me.

One day, I thought, if we trouble these great creatures too

much, and hack away at them and destroy their young, they will simply uproot themselves and march away, whole forests on the move, over the next range and next, far from the haunts of man. I have seen many forests and green places dwindle and disappear. Now there is an outcry. It is suddenly fashionable to be an environmentalist. That's all right. Perhaps, it is not too late to save the little that is left.

By and large, writers have to stay in the plains to make a living. Hill people have their work cut out trying to wrest a livelihood from their thin, calcinated soil. And as for mountaineers, they climb their peaks and move on in search of other peaks.

But to me, as a writer, mountains have been kind. They were kind from the beginning, when I left a job in Delhi and rented a small cottage on the outskirts of the hill station. Today, most hill stations are rich men's playgrounds, but years ago they were places where people of modest means would live quite cheaply. There were few cars and everyone walked about.

The cottage was on the edge of an oak and maple forest and I spent eight or nine years in it, most of them happy, writing stories, essays, poems and books for children. I think this had something to do with Prem's children. He and his wife had taken on the job of looking after the house and all practical matters (I remain helpless with fuses, clogged cisterns, leaking gas cylinders, ruptured water pipes, tin roofs that blow away when there is a storm, and the do-it-yourself world of small-town India).

Naturally, I grew attached to them and became a part of the family, an adopted grandfather. For Rakesh, I wrote a story about a cherry tree that had difficulty in growing up. For Mukesh, who liked upheavals, I wrote a story about an earthquake and put him in it, and for Dolly, I wrote rhymes.

'Who goes to the Hills, goes to his Mother,' wrote Kipling, and he seldom wrote truer words. For living in the hills was like living in the bosom of a strong, sometimes proud, but always a comforting mother. And every time I went away, the homecoming would be tender and precious. It became increasingly difficult for me to go away.

It has not always been happiness and light though. There were times when money ran out. Editorial doors sometimes close; but when one door closes another has, for me, almost immediately, miraculously opened.

When you have received love from people and the freedom that only mountains can give, then you have come very near the borders of Heaven.

LIGHT SUPPERS MAKE LONG LIVES

O range and lemons. They were always on my grandmother's dining table, in preference to creamy cakes and puddings. She was frugal in matters pertaining to food, and disapproved of small boys with large appetites. If I wanted something more substantial than a lemon I'd have to sneak over to her tenant, old Miss Kellner, a cripple from childhood, who would ply me with meringues and nankatties, soft creamy biscuits obtained from a local baker.

'Oranges,' proclaimed Granny, 'are good for the complexion, and lemons good for the digestion.'

She was probably right, because she had a flawless complexion and lived to be eighty without too many internal problems.

Oranges were cheap—so much so, that I remember attending a Test cricket match during which the crowd flung oranges on to the ground because they were dissatisfied with the home team's performance. A waste of good fruit but better than throwing bottles.

To return to Granny and her views on eating, I remember that she had at her command a number of kitchen proverbs (some of them her own) which she would direct at me whenever I asked for a second helping.

'Better a small fish than an empty dish,' was one of them. And another went, 'Light suppers make for long lives.' Looking back, I can accept the truth of these maxims, but at the time I was all in favour of large fish and substantial suppers.

Another kitchen proverb went, 'Don't let your tongue cut you throat,' directed at me whenever I was guilty of overeating. It could also be used if I talked too much.

'Don't waste words,' said Granny. 'Speak only when spoken to.'

So instead of speaking my words, and finding that no one wanted to listen to them, I began putting them down on paper. Viola! There they were, in my own handwriting, and short of tearing them up no one could make them vanish.

◆

Today, kind people ply me with cakes, chocolates and desi sweets. I am at an age when I am quite indifferent to these things. A small fish will do. But I remember the hungry years, when I was in my early twenties, living alone, an unknown writer, with no one to send me candies and wine. I could have done with a few of these luxuries in those far-off days. But when you are a nobody, no one sends you presents. Such is the irony of life.

At the age of nineteen I was living on my own in London and working as an accounts clerk. It took at least 45 minutes for me to reach the office by the tube train. Often, afraid of being late, I'd skip breakfast, as breakfast was something I'd have to make myself. During the lunch break I'd walk over to a snack bar and order baked beans on toast, the cheapest item on the menu. Sometimes a fellow clerk would share his marmite sandwiches with me. Good old marmite, you could live on it for months! And in the evening, I'd treat myself to a 'light supper' at a small café, and occasionally I'd indulge in a glass of sherry. South African sherry was the cheapest, 2s.6d for a bottle; cheaper than beer. After two years of this rigorous diet I ended up in hospital suffering from severe malnutrition.

When I had saved up enough money, I returned to India, where there was always 'dal-bhaath' for lunch, and a paratha for breakfast, even in the most difficult times. And some sweet lime pickle to go with it. Granny was right. Lemons are good for the digestion.

◆

As Christmas and the New Year approaches, I am sometimes asked for my memories of past celebrations. Alas, I have to say that we never celebrated on a grand scale. Funds were tight, with my grandmother and then with my mother and stepfather. Oddly enough, the most memorable Christmas that I can remember was celebrated in the State of Jamnagar where my father conducted a small palace school for the girls and younger children of the royal family. The Maharaja (or Jam-Sahib as he had called) was a kind soul who showered gifts on the children of the State's employees during Christmas and Diwali. I was there till the age of six, and I vividly remember being given toys, books, confectionary in abundance.

The Jam-Sahib had also given refuge to hundreds of Polish families who had fled after Hitler's invasion of their homeland. The State or Jamnagar took care of them throughout the duration of World War II. This was not at generosity that is forgotten here but still remembered in Poland.

Jamnagar was also the home of Indian cricket. Earlier rulers included Ranjitsinhji and his nephew Duleepsinhji, both stylish batsmen who played regularly for England in their heyday. The State also gave us that great all-rounder Vinoo Mankad, who was the mainstay of the Indian Test team in the early 1950s. Descendants of the ruling Jadeja family still play for India.

The Jam-Sahib often invited English cricket teams to play in the state, and I remember being taken along to one of these matches. I don't remember any of the cricket, but I do remember the dishes of sweets that were continually being passed around in the pavilion, and I focused (with great success) on rasgullas, gulab jamuns, laddoos and jalebis.

Alas, all this ended when my father joined the R.A.F., and I was sent to a boarding school in the hills. The fare consisted of pumpkins and boiled mutton and a tasteless custard pudding. Then my father died and hard times were upon us, culminating in that lonely and debilitating period in England. London must have been the loneliest city in the world for a nineteen-year-old without friends or family.

It was wonderful to come back to India. Facing a little hardship here were easy because so many young people were facing hardship too. The only thing I could do well was to put words down on paper and try to bring them to life. I've been doing it for over sixty years. In India, the pen cannot run dry. Something is happening all the time.

So, this has become something of a mini-autobiography appropriate, perhaps, as another year draws to a close.

There are good times and there are bad times, but one must never forget the hard times. Who knows, they might come again. So, 'Be prepared!' as the Boy Scouts motto goes.

As I was finding this essay, Beera (my granddaughter) came into the room and asked me what I'd like for lunch. Absent-mindedly I replied: 'Baked beans on toast.' Granny would have approved.